C000054689

NOTHING WOULD
MAKE ME HAPPIER

Christy Smyth

Plastic Brain Press

Horncastle
Lincolnshire
United Kingdom

plasticbrainpress@gmail.com

www.plastic-brain-press.com

Copyright © 2021 Christy Smyth

First published in Great Britain in 2021

All rights reserved.

No part of this publication may be produced, stored in a retrieval system, or transmitted, in any form or by any means without the prior written permission of the publisher, not be otherwise circulated in any form of binding or cover or print other than that in which it is published and without a similar condition being imposed on the subsequent purchaser. All characters in this publication are fictitious and any resemblance to real persons, living or dead, is purely coincidental.

ISBN-13: 978-1-8381667-1-7

Cover design: Melody Clark

Copyright © 2021 by Christy Smyth

CONTENTS

THE CARDS YOU'RE DEALT

A boy from year nine runs up and down the sixth form car park. He asks the same question to every student he meets.

"Hey, Dom, did you hear about Jizzstain? Hey, Eddy, did you hear about Jizzstain? Hey, Sabatina, did you hear about Jizzstain?"

Finally the boy makes his way to Natalie.

"Have you heard, Nathan?"

"You know what my name is, so get it fucking right."

"Not gonna tell you now, am I?"

The idea of anyone at Atlantic Academy knowing something she doesn't makes Natalie's skin crawl. Her little sister, Bunny, says she's allergic to minding her own business. She lunges forward to grab the year nine, but he ducks out the way and makes a run for it. She chases him in circles for a while before she manages to grab him by the collar of his too-big blazer and pin him against the passenger door of Everest Branham's car.

"Shitting hell!" Everest cries, jumping out and shoving the boy aside to make sure there's no damage to his vehicle.

"This little twat won't tell me what's gone on with Jizzstain."

"He only went and pissed in the fountain."

"That's hysterical." Natalie says, though her expression doesn't change and she talks through gritted teeth.

"Yeah, I mean it wasn't *that* cool. He just pissed in a crisp packet and poured it in."

"What flavour?"

"Why does that matter?"

The bell rings and Everest turns to leave.

"Have you seen Isla?" Natalie calls after him.

"Not today. She was with Karen at the Castle last night."

When she gets to Mr Cahill's Ethics class and sees that Isla's seat is empty, Natalie knows that something is awfully wrong. Isla never misses Mr Cahill's classes. Even when Isla is ill, Natalie will video call her and prop the phone up against a text book. But Isla hasn't returned any of Natalie's calls or texts today.

"Oi, Karen," Natalie whispers, "Karen. Oi. Oi. Karen. Karen. Oi." She scrunches up a piece of paper and throws it across the room. Still no response. "What have I done to deserve the silent treatment?"

Karen doesn't flinch. She looks straight on at Mr Cahill, who sits on his desk at the front of the class, swinging his little legs to and fro, arguing with himself. He speaks to the class in his own peculiar way. He drags his sentences out until words turn into unintelligible croaks, gathers his breath, and starts again.

"Today we'll be talking about euthanaaasia." As he exhales he slumps forward, then pulls himself back up. "One of the most difficult ethical issues you can faaace."

He writes 'DEATH WITH DIGNITY' in large letters on the whiteboard and turns to look at his students. No one looks back with equal gravity.

"Can I get a volunteer to read out the opening passage from the sheeet?"

Someone in the room makes a revolting gurgling sound, followed by a rattle and choke. All heads turn to look at Karen, who grips the sides of her desk with all her might, tears streaming down her face.

"Kaaaren! What's wrooong?"

Karen has turned deathly pale. She releases her grip only to claw at the pages of her textbook. She lets out an ear-piercing shriek, frantically wails as though in unimaginable pain and struggles for breath between guttural moans and groans. Mr Cahill watches on, sweating, desperately hoping he hasn't unlocked some suppressed trauma.

Before he has a chance to say anything else, he is saved by an announcement coming over the tannoy.

"Can Karen Hurst come to Mr Erickson's office right away."

"Natalie, can you accompany Kaaaren?"

Natalie takes the inconsolable girl by the arm and leads her out the room while the rest of the class watch on, their mouths and eyes open wide. That is except Jizzstain, who hasn't been paying attention. He stares out the window and quietly wonders whether they could pull DNA evidence from the prawn cocktail crisp packet he left floating in the fountain.

Bunny sits outside Mr Erickson's office, arms folded, pouting.

"What happened to you?" Natalie asks.

"What? Oh. Hey. Uh, I was just. You know. I don't know. Mrs Nettle said I had to come here. What's up with her?"

Karen has calmed somewhat. She's stopped screaming. She's gurgling again, letting the tears run down her cheeks.

"I don't fucking know, do I? When you went to the Castle last night was Isla there?"

"What? Oh. Uh. No. I don't think so."

"I'm gonna head down there now. You wanna come?"

"Can we, uh, you know? Make a detour? Stop off at home?"

"No."

"Oh. OK. I'll come anyway."

***

Angel Darling lives in The Castle, an enormous pink mansion that stands in stark contrast to the bungalows that surround it. The Castle was brought for her by her husband. He's an orthodontist, and a distant relative to the Queen. If some unprecedented disaster were to hit the royal family, Angel might become Princess Angel Darling.

Bunny knows better than to ring the buzzer at the gates and risk getting through to the help. Instead, she suggests they walk around the back and scale the wall.

There's a boy Natalie recognises as Everest Branham's little brother, Bertie, stood under a tree in the gardens. He looks desperate to leave, repeatedly reaching down to lift apples from a wheelbarrow. Angel is stood twenty yards away, holding a cricket bat.

"Get a move on, Bertie, or I'll have that quart back."

The boy picks out an apple and expertly throws it towards Angel. She swings and misses. They repeat the process several times over before she manages to clip one, tearing it to pieces.

"Superb!" Angel sequels. She seems to notice Natalie and Bunny, but says nothing as she walks leisurely to where Bertie stands. She hands him the bat and pats him on the arse before the boy walks back to the house. She then turns to the girls and gives them a wide smile, showing off several gaps where prominent teeth should be. It's no secret that the royal orthodontist likes to bring his work to the bedroom.

"Hey gals, what can I do you for?"

"Have you seen Isla?"

"Yeah, her and Karen were here last night. They didn't stick around long, though. Why do you ask? She gone AWOL again?"

"She didn't show for Ethics with Cahill."

"Oh dear. Well, you're in luck, because I've got just the thing to help you find her."

They walk through what seems to Natalie like a hundred hallways to get to Angel's 'spiritual sanctuary'. They sit around a table that's covered by a fringed cloth which Angel said she inherited from her grandmother. She removes the rose quartz obelisk, and replaces it with amethyst, as well as an arrangement of white and pink flowers.

Angel lifts a cardboard box from the corner of the room and shows the girls what's inside; a hundred smaller boxes, each labelled 'Miss Angel Darling's Angel Cards'.

"They just came the other day," she says, "I was thinking I could sell them at that market in Kennford."

"Oh, uh, right. I don't know about this."

"Yeah, that Tarot shit freaks me out."

"That's the great thing about Angel Cards! They focus on the positives. Here, Natalie, shuffle these. It'll help you find Isla, I'm sure of it."

Natalie shuffles and keeps an eye on Angel, waiting for a sign to tell her when to stop. Angel gestures for her to spread them out on the table.

"Pick three out and put them face down in front of you. Follow your heart."

Natalie follows the instructions. As she puts the last card down, Angel takes a deep breath, then turns them over one by one, reading out the messages as she goes.

"'Endurance. The angels acknowledge your troubles, and admire your persistent ability to overcome them. You are a strong, powerful person. These are traits that come naturally to you, which may cause jealousy in others. You mustn't let this affect your progress. Your affirmation is, *I can do everything. I can overcome anything, I can feel nothing.*'"

"Uh, I don't know if it's a good idea to feel *nothing*."

"No, it means nothing can hurt you. That's a good thing. Here, let's look at the next one. 'Petulance. The angels recognise your occasional ill-temper. It disappoints them. You are a child at heart, but this is holding you back. Don't be afraid of growing up. With time, all petty differences fade away. Your affirmation is, *It's never too late, until it is*.'"

"I don't have an ill-temper."

"Uh, actually, you kinda do. In fact, it's probably your, uh, defining trait."

"Fuck you!"

"I don't really remember writing that one. It does seem a bit much. Never mind, one more. This will unlock the key to Isla's whereabouts, I can feel it. 'Ignorance. The angels think you are a bad person and they don't like you. They think you're obnoxious and rude. They talk about you behind your back. You are unattractive. You smell. You are very ill and you don't know it. Your ambitions will never come to fruition. You have no affirmation. You don't deserve one.'"

"What the fuck, Angel?"

"I definitely didn't write that."

"That wasn't very fucking positive."

"There must have been a mix up or something."

"Come on, Bunny, maybe Bash has heard from Isla."

Angel rises quickly from her seat, knocking over a burning incense stick which Bunny manages to stamp out.

"Don't go. I've got other stuff. We can get stoned and watch *Ancient Aliens*."

"Uh, yeah, that sounds cool, but, uh, maybe another time."

As the two girls leave, Angel slumps back into her chair. She looks around at all of her things and feels something close to nothing at all.

***

Ever since Bosh's wife left him two years ago, his curtain-twitching neighbours have been exchanging theories as to why it is that so many teenagers turn up at his house. Tim Wise from 43 even sprayed the word 'nonce' on his garage door. It's still there.

Bosh's weasel-faced son, Bash, answers the door, looking dazed and a little upset. He has a yellow hue to his skin and the expression of a confused infant.

"Ladies," he says, matter-of-factly, "Wanna hear my idea for a movie?"

"Is Isla about?"

"I've not seen her, but you can come in and ask around."

Natalie follows Bash inside, but Bunny hesitates.

"Um, Natalie, if we're gonna be, you know, hanging about... And, uh, our house is only down the road, so... Can I grab..."

"For fuck's sake, Bunny, go on then!"

Natalie and Bash walk straight through to the kitchen. The window is broken and partially open at all times. Not enough to let out all the smoke. Bash returns to his seat at the family table, which has the names of every stoner in town carved into it. Bosh sits to his left, wearing only a pair of pants, and Bish to his right, who should be in school and wears the same uniform as Natalie. There are cards laid out on the table and arranged into different spreads. Bish doesn't look up from his own cards as he raises a hand in greeting. He's twitching and shuffling in his seat. Bosh, meanwhile, leans back in his chair, dirty bare feet on the table and a smug grin on his face. In the centre of the table is a large glass jar filled with damiana, and the boys are passing two joints around. Bash offers one to Natalie, who takes it only to read what's written on the Rizla. It's a tradition between Bish and Bash to name their joints. They add each name to a list they've kept since they were both fourteen. It spans two notebooks. This one is called, 'Arthur Brown'.

"Did you have your turn, then?" Bash asks.

"It was your turn! It was his turn, wasn't it, dad?"

Bish is Bosh's step-son, and Bash his son from his first marriage. Bish was given the option to leave with his mother, but he never cared much for Christine and she never cared much for him. He had this much in common with Bosh, so he stuck around. The nicknames are used to avoid confusion, as they all share the name Wilfred.

"Whatever," Bosh says, taking his feet off the table and sitting upright. "I'm having my turn."

Bish looks on indignantly as Bosh moves a card on the table from one pile to another and puts one down from his own hand.

"'Inescapable Nightmare: If the table's Horror Count is greater than nine and someone has Gnawing Doubt, the game wins'."

"But no one has Gnawing Doubt," Bish says.

"I thought Bash had it?"

"I got rid of that, like, three turns ago. Anyway, the Horror Count is only at seven."

"Whatever. I can't keep up with this."

"Have either of you seen Isla?"

"Hey, dad, you wanna hear my idea for a movie?"

Bunny returns and everyone watches as she shuffles through the hall and into the kitchen. She's changed into her outfit. It's getting to be too small for her now, but she stuffs herself in. One ear flops at the side of her head and the pink of the fabric is fading. The suit is all-encompassing, other than the small circle of her face.

"You boys playing *Madness & Misery*? Mind if I join?"

She sits at the table and takes a tin from the zipper pocket at her hip. From the tin she takes her roach card, weed, and orange liquorice papers, leaving the tobacco, choosing instead to take a generous pinch of the damiana from the glass jar. The boys watch on as she rolls one of her signature joints, long and thick enough to look like a carrot.

"Hey, Bunny, wanna hear my idea for a movie?"

Bosh rolls his eyes.

"So there's this woman, right. Just a regular old woman. I mean, she's not *old*. Like, mid-40s. And she works at a chippy. Just a regular chippy, right. But what she really wants is to be a detective. She's wanted to be a detective since she was a little kid, you know? So one day this customer walks in. He's in there all the time. And he says, 'Hey, Gale—"

"Gale?"

"Yeah, that's her name."

"The detective?"

"No. I mean, yes, but she's not a detective. She's just a chip shop woman."

"So what's the detectives' name? Could it be Lance Hollander?"

"There is no detective! It's just Gale and the customer. And he's just a normal guy."

"Lance Hollander could be a normal guy. I knew a Lance Peterson. He was a normal guy."

"Do you mean Lance Patterson? He wasn't a normal guy, dad. He killed his wife. And her lover!"

"The man is called Dave, OK? So Dave comes in and, uh, Gale, she says to him, 'Hey, Dave, you want your Spam fritters?'"

"What?"

"That's disgusting."

"You're sick, Bash. You're sick in the head!"

"Dave likes Spam Fritters, OK? It's called character building. Like you'd know anything about writing you fucking illiterate."

Bish pulls a face and goes back to writing 'Lance Hollander' onto a Rizla.

"So, anyway, before Dave can even answer he falls to the floor and whatshername, uh, Gale, she sees he's got blood all on his shirt and shit and he's just there dying on the floor of this chip shop."

"Oh, shit."

"I know! So Gale gets to thinking, like, this old guy, he's just a regular old guy. So she thought. But here he is, like he's been shot or stabbed or something."

"Wait a minute, didn't someone get stabbed outside The Village Fryer last week? That was an old guy, right?"

"Well I wouldn't use his real name or anything. And I've put in the whole detective thing!"

"For fuck's sake, I've had enough of this. Come on, Bunny, let's see if she's at Big Lad's."

"Oh yeah. That's probably where she is. But wait, Bash, does the detective solve the case?"

"Uh, I dunno. I guess not. You know, she's not a real detective. She's just a chip shop woman. And that's all she'll ever be."

"That's sad, man."

***

Big Lad lives on the seventh floor of Ayer Court. Natalie and Bunny listen to the whirr of the elevator as it ascends and descends but never opens for them. They eventually decide to take the stairs, and see that a tattooed man is filling the lift with boxes on the second floor, taking them up to the sixth, then going back down to get more. Natalie rings the personalised door bell that sounds the opening theme from *The Generation Game* while Bunny pants, sweating in her suit. There's lots of whispering, shuffling, and grunting before the door opens. Big Lad is a big lad. He wears a blue dressing gown, fluffy fox slippers, and a key on a piece of string around his neck. He's as breathless as Bunny.

"Oh, mate, am I glad to see you!"

"Hey, B.L." Bunny wheezes.

"Oh, boy! Oh, mate! What a fucking day! Crazy! You wouldn't believe it! Really!"

Bunny goes straight through to the sink to get water while Natalie looks around for somewhere to sit. Her options are limited. It's a tiny flat, with much of the space taken up by a king size bed with an inordinate amount of pillows. There's stacks of books piled high with everything from religious texts to *Idiot's Guides*. *Beyond Good And Evil*, *The Illuminated Blake*, the 1997 *Viz* annual. Natalie decides to perch on top of a stack of thick *Taschen* books on art and architecture. She's trying hard not to sneeze from the combined scents of cannabis and cannabis incense.

In the corner of the room is a tank with two fish. Even they look stoned. They float in one corner, gormlessly staring at a castle made of colourful pebbles.

"Boy, I sure am glad you're here!"

Big Lad has to shout over the noise from all the flats around him. He's been shouting for years now. It's become his standard register. There's an extremely pale, ginger boy who lives alone upstairs. He spends all day playing video games with the volume at full blast, listening to late-career Eminem, and censoring his own curses. Then there's the woman next door who has a vacuum going at all times. She says she needs it to help her sleep, and she's always sleeping. Across the hall is someone who Big Lad has never seen, but who has a cat that seems to be in constant heat, crying out and scratching at the door.

Of course, Big Lad is a noisy neighbour himself, always listening to *The Rambunctious Rico Show.* He's a regular caller, and often likes to bring up the fact that he was an early fan, back when Rico only had a two hour slot. Now he's on sixteen hours a day, with Restrained Rodney taking over for the eight hours that Rico spends in bed.

"Really, I'm really very very glad to see you! It's been a day! A day and a half! Two days in one day, almost!"

The boy playing his video game upstairs is shooting something and laughing.

"Have it you sugaring effers! You ruddy effs!"

"Your mate Isla was here this morning!"

"Finally. We've been looking all over for her."

"What?"

"What is he saying?"

"He says Isla was here this morning."

"Well it's about time. We've been looking all over for her."

"Looking for who?"

The woman next door bangs on the wall.

"Keep it down in there, some of us are trying to sleep."

"I said your mate Isla was here this morning! With her boyfriend! Whatshisname!

"Nick was here too?"

"No! Isla! Isla was here with that guy! Uh, Nick? They were here for hours! I got this new game where you gotta fight this giant wasp! It's impossible, man! Crazy! You wanna play?"

"What?"

"I said Isla was here with Nick for hours!"

"Yeah?"

"Then I said I got this new game where you gotta fight this giant wasp! It's impossible!"

"Yeah?"

"Then I asked if you wanted to play!"

"What's B.L. saying?"

A computerised explosion goes off upstairs and the boy throws his controller.

"You f-words! You effing f-words!"

"You hear this guy?! Crazy! Just crazy!"

"Do you know where Isla is now?"

"She was here this morning! With Nick! We were playing Rummy! Her idea! I didn't even know how to play Rummy! Neither did Nick! She had to spend hours teaching us! We were so stoned, man! It was crazy!"

"He's saying Isla was getting them to play Rummy."

"Always with the Rummy."

"What?"

"For fuck's sake, Big Lad, turn the fucking radio off!"

"Hey effs, cool it with the effing profanities down there!"

Big Lad silences Rambunctious Rico while he's part way through talking to a nurse from Chichester about the DAS.

"Hey, I just remembered, I ordered a Chinese! You guys want a Chinese? I can call the Chinaman if you like?"

Natalie shakes her head and reaches over for another couple of books so she can sit more comfortably.

"You sure? It's good stuff! Crazy good! I got a Singapore Chow Mein! You ever have that?"

"So where's Isla now?" Bunny asks, tapping on the tank but getting no reaction from the fish.

"She started freaking out! Crazy! So Nick took her home! She was totally freaking out! Just hysterical! She was crying! Like, really crying! Just crazy and hysterical!"

"So they went back to hers or what?"

"He took her home but then he came back! That's the thing! That's what's so crazy! He's still here!"

There's a sudden cracking sound, and the room goes quiet. The vacuum stops humming and the cat stops scratching. Big Lad tries flicking a light switch but it doesn't work.

He tries turning the TV on but nothing happens. They're left with the sound of low moaning coming from the bathroom, something that had been inaudible before.

"That's him! He started freaking out too so I had to lock him in!"

"Why do you have a lock on the outside?"

"Are you sure you don't want a Chinese? It's good stuff! Crazy good!"

"Can we see him?"

"That's the thing! I wanted to check in on him but I can't find the key!"

Another cracking sound brings back the noise. The vacuum starts up. The boy returns to his game. The cat scratches and cries.

Then there's a knock at Big Lad's front door.

"It's the Chinaman!"

Big Lad goes to answer the door, then stops and slaps his head in a cartoonish display of realisation.

"The key is around my neck! The key was on my neck all along!"

He turns back to the bathroom but is interrupted by another knock at the door.

"Oh, shit! Hold on Nick, I've just got to get this!"

He reaches for the door handle, but stops to slap his head again.

"The money! I need the money! Can you see where I put the money?"

He starts looking around all the surfaces, but is distracted by a thumping sound from the bathroom.

"Nick! Oh shit, do you think he's alright? Let's get him out of there!"

Another knock.

"Just one moment! I'll be right there!"

All the while, Natalie stays seated on her book pile, and Bunny feeds the fish. Big Lad manages to get the bathroom door open, and they all see Nick, curled up in the foetal position, making strange gurgling and rattling sounds. The man at the door is knocking over and over.

"Answer your effing door!"

Natalie sighs before getting up and opening the front door. The delivery boy is small and rotund. His head and body are perfectly round. His arms are straight by his side and his feet point outwards. He looks like a child's drawing of a person. He sees the girl in the bunny outfit, the bald giant and the teenage boy moaning on the floor. Then he looks at Natalie and says something unbelievably funny. An off-the-cuff remark, perfectly timed and delivered. A punchline so good, it would have you laughing for weeks.

Natalie looks back at him confused. She doesn't speak the language.

DADDY, NO

Derek still dreams of the ordinance plant, though he's never seen it in real life. The ordinance plant of his dreams is a surreal approximation built from descriptions in safety information guidebooks. Here, it is an impossibly enormous building. He stands in a glass box suspended from the ceiling, watching the woman at work, noting each error in her process.

"Take off your shoes!" He cries. "We're at 20% humidity, you bitch!"

Lena can't hear him. She never can. Time and time again she makes the same mistakes.

Derek never met Lena in real life. The Lena of his dreams is an unrealistically beautiful snapshot built from photographs seen in magazines and news segments. She performs her tasks in an uncanny, robotic manner. She smiles, blissfully unaware of her inevitable fate.

"No, no, no! You've got to wait fifteen minutes! Don't go in there!"

At this point, as always, everything slows down. A mushroom cloud forms and envelopes Lena. She is a woman made of fire.

Her smile shatters as bits of tooth and tongue fly off in all directions like shrapnel. Even with her body torn to pieces, her agonised screams still echo through the building.

Derek stands in his glass box, filled with an overwhelming sense of disappointment. He folds his arms and shakes his head.

"See, that's what you get."

"What?"

Derek sits upright in his bed. The room feels unfamiliar. He looks out the window at the London sky, and it all comes rushing back.

"Did you say something?" Brad asks.

"What are you accusing me of?"

Derek gets out of bed before Brad has a chance to answer.

They've lived here a month, and have little to show for it. The walls are a featureless cream, the living room has only two deck chairs and a broken TV. The kitchen is filled with empty pizza boxes and uncleaned mugs. Derek boils the kettle and briefly listens to the radio until Rambunctious Rico starts fielding calls about Top Notch and the protests at the courthouse. He can't stand to hear about it anymore. That's why he broke the TV.

Just as he turns the radio off, Derek's phone rings. Seeing it's an unfamiliar number, he braces himself.

"Is that Johnny Little-Hart?"

It takes Derek a moment to switch gears as his anxiety turns to excitement.

"It's Ben from Sadsac. I know it's last minute, but would you be able to make it in for a meeting this afternoon?"

He sounds on the verge of tears. Derek knows this can only be a good sign.

Even in Ben's small, grey office, Derek can hear the weeping. It comes from both the editors next door and the funeral directors downstairs. He sits on a red plastic chair that seems more suited to a primary school. The room smells damp and looks like it's falling apart. There's torn wallpaper and black mould and a standing fan that rattles and shakes.

Ben sits opposite Derek. He wears a creased white shirt and a black tie that he compulsively adjusts and readjusts and sometimes uses to dry his wet eyes. He's surrounded by manuscript pages and balled up tissues.

"Bare with me one moment," he says, gathering stacks of paper, occasionally catching glimpses of what is written on them and choking up. "Oh dear. Oh no. Oh, you poor thing." He puts them aside and takes another manuscript out of his drawer: *Daddy, No* by Johnny Little-Hart.

"So, is Johnny a pen name?"

"Yes, sorry, my real—"

"Johnny, please, there's no need to apologise. Now, I'm going to be straight with you. We're not going to be able to publish your book."

Behind Ben is a window, through which Derek can see the editors at work. One of them, a young man with the thin, white hair of someone much older, holds a small paperback in one hand, and uses his other to cover his mouth as he heaves and wretches.

"Put simply, *Daddy, No* is just too light, too... feel-good. Sure, there are some striking moments. The beatings, the basements, the abandonments. The bit where your dad keeps you in a drawer. It's fine work, but you've got to understand that this is stuff we see every day."

The white-haired editor brings the paperback to a colleague, who looks it over and appears to have an instant panic attack. They both weep and hold each other reassuringly.

"I mean, look at something like *Silent Cries (From Blackened Eyes)*. You know, by Richard Moody? Over a million copies sold. The first time I read that, I tell you, I couldn't come into work for a week. Now *that's* what I call depressing."

"Sorry, I—"

"Johnny, I told you once, as long as you're in this office, you never have to apologise. Here at a Sadsac we're all about forgiveness and redemption. And sometimes revenge."

The white-haired editor moves to a tall window, threatening to jump, while three of his co-workers urge him to reconsider and a fourth arranges a three book deal with the author of the paperback.

"Right. But, I just want to make sure we're on the same page."

"It's not just this page, Johnny. It's *this* page and *that* page. I mean, there are whole chapters here that are practically happy-go-lucky."

The white-haired editor finally steps back from the window and returns to his desk, where he blows his nose, dries his eyes, and picks up another book.

"You're saying there's no chance?"

"Not unless your life gets any worse."

A small group of people weep in a huddle by the reception desk. It takes only a moment for Derek to recognise the man they surround. Richard Moody wears sunglasses and chews gum. He bares his yellow teeth as he smiles, patting the fans reassuringly on the back. Derek wants to leave but can't get past the huddle to the lift. He takes a seat beside an elderly man who reads a magazine called *Tygodnik Przegląd.* The man appears to recognise Derek, and mutters something

Slavic-sounding before going back to his reading.

Derek hasn't seen Richard in several years. Not in real life. Only on daytime TV, promoting one or other of his several volumes of miserable memoirs.

"My son!" He suddenly cries, signing one last book. "My lovely, lovely son! What are *you* doing here?"

Derek stands up and allows his father to embrace his limp body.

"I just had a meeting about my book."

"Your book? Oh, my son! My sweet, innocent, son! Whatever would *you* have to write about?"

Richard notices the manuscript under Derek's arm, and on seeing the title, clutches his heart in an exaggerated display of incredulity. "Oh! Oh, son of mine! Sweet boy! Sweet, sweet, darling, innocent boy! What is this all about? Sure, I knocked you around a little, but come on! Is this to do with keeping you in that drawer? Because we've talked about that. It was a big drawer!"

"Mr Moody," the receptionist interrupts, "Ben is ready for you now."

Suddenly Ben bursts through the door with a bottle of champagne in one hand and a box of tissues in the other.

"Moody, my man! You must read this book. It's by some Polish bloke whose daughter got blown up. I think you're in for some competition!"

Before Derek knows what to say, Richard disappears into Ben's office, and he is left with the magazine-reading old man and the red-eyed receptionist who examines her newly signed copy of *Silent Cries (From Blackened Eyes)*.

On the reception desk, Derek sees a card with his father's contact details. He doesn't want it, but he takes it all the same.

Derek gently spins in his swivel chair, keeping an eye on the screen of his laptop, as though the words might appear at any moment. Post-it notes cover the walls, accompanied by pictures of Derek as a child. The photos show the boy in progressing stages of misery, from pout to weep to wail. Now and then he scrolls through the document, examining passages. He reaches back into the darkest recesses of his memory, desperate to find something terrible he might have suppressed. He tries using different, more aggressive adjectives to describe the people and places, but each time ends up clicking 'undo'. It's been two hours like this and nothing has changed.

On a cork board, between a hand drawn family tree and a review of *Silent Cries* cut from an issue of *Tragedy Magazine*, is a newspaper advertisement from the 90s for a chest of drawers. It is noted just how much they can hold.

"You won't be too long, will you?" Brad asks from the doorway. "You'll only upset yourself."

It is in this moment that the idea comes to him. And as Brad shuts the office door, Derek gets to work. He closes the document on his laptop and in its place, opens up a series of tabs, preparing the individual pages so that he is able to complete each task in quick succession. First he cancels the direct debit for the council tax, then the rent, the landline, the gas and the electric. He cancels the Netflix and the Spotify and the PornHub Premium. To add insult to injury, he donates what is left of his severance payment to a fundraiser dedicated to covering the legal fees of Top Notch. This, he thinks, will surely have some awful karmic repercussions. He makes new plans to fill his days. He decides to start taking late night trips to Dagenham, Neasden and West Ealing, around Uxbridge Road. Maybe he'll try some hard drugs. Maybe he'll take up drinking heavily. Surely Brad will leave him. If he's really lucky, Brad will admit he never loved him at all. Finally, he takes the card out of his pocket, dials the number, and leaves a polite message with an invitation to dinner.

Derek goes to bed, trying hard to suppress giggles of excitement, knowing soon he would have some brilliantly devastating and devastatingly brilliant material for his memoir. And that night, as Lena burns in his dreams, Derek shakes his head and says,

"You think that's bad? You should read my book!"

Brad and Alberta sit shirtless on the floor, Poundland candles arranged in a circle around them. Seated, Alberta is almost as tall as Brad is standing. Derek watches them from the doorway. They don't notice his presence. Their eyes are closed.

"I see a corridor," Alberta says, "at the end of which is a red door. To the left of the red door is a blue door. More periwinkle than powder. To the right of the red door is a green door."

"I wish to open the blue door."

Alberta motions, as if tentatively taking hold of the imagined handle, then pushes it open.

"Ah! Behind the aforementioned blue door, again, I must be clear, more periwinkle than powder, is a woman. Her hair is long. She is young, but not very young. She is sad, but not very sad."

"I wish to ask the woman her name."

"L- Lil- Lilly? Lillian? L- Laura?"

"Lena?"

"Lena! Yes! Lena, do you wish to speak?"

Derek rolls his eyes and walks through to the kitchen. Alerted by the sudden movement, Brad lets go of Alberta's wrists which, in turn, causes her to choke and gasp for breath.

"The circle is broken!"

Derek struggles to watch Brad in these sessions with their neighbour. Not least because his shirtlessness gives away his strange shape. Brad's head is big, and his body immensely muscular, but he has short, sparrow legs that don't seem at all strong enough to support his weight.

"Derek! We were just getting somewhere! I'm so sorry, Alberta."

"You should have more respect for the circle, Mr Derek."

Alberta doesn't open her eyes as she removes a pair of comically large sunglasses from the front pocket of her purple tuxedo and a pack of slim Vogues from the inside.

"Please don't smoke in here."

"It's all a part of the process, Mr Derek."

She blows out a single candle, then puts one hand on her head and keeps it there.

"We will have to wait for the negative powertrons to disperse before we attempt to reconstruct the circle."

"Don't worry," Derek says, "I'll be gone soon." He rummages around, looking for his keys as Alberta taps on the walls with her long, dirty nails.

"You did right to move here. I sense good fortune awaiting you both."

As Derek leaves the flat, he hears the familiar voice of his father. Alberta has left the radio blaring in her room across the hall.

"It was, undoubtably, the hardest thing I've ever had to write." Richard says.

"Harder even. Than the chapter from. *Gently Sobbing, Sobbing Gently*. With the cactus. And the Custard Cream?"

"Well, Rico, writing that certainly did bring up a lot of painful memories. To this day I struggle to look a Custard Cream in the eye. Or even a Bourbon."

"Or. Even. A. Bourbon. Powerful stuff."

The sound of Derek's father is interrupted by heavy footsteps coming up the stairs, followed by Magnus' booming voice.

"Oi, oi!"

This is a more welcome greeting than Derek is used to. Magnus is usually a more intimidating figure. He's enormous, with a spine-chilling mullet and a wide-eyed, unhinged expression. He spent many years behind bars when he killed a nun, just for the thrill of it.

"I was hoping to see you." He says. "I've heard we have a mutual friend. Well, myself and Mr Notch are particularly grateful. So much so that this month the milky bars are on me, if you know what I mean?"

He doesn't know what Magnus means, but before he has time to respond, the landlord has continued on his journey to the next floor, and Derek is alone again. He tunes back in to the muffled sounds of Rambunctious Rico.

"Next up we have. Kacper Symanski. Whose new book. Also published through. Sadsac Press. Tells the story of. His daughter who. Died. Tragically. And lived. Much the same."

"That part where your dad put your hand in the toaster and toasted it and then spread butter on your hand and made you try and eat it? That was just awful!"

"You know, it wasn't even butter? It was 'I Can't Believe It's Not Butter'."

"I can't believe it!"

"Well, I've eaten worse."

"If *Recipe For Abuse* was anything to go by, I can only imagine."

Brad is meeting Richard for the first time. He's only ever been allowed to read a handful of passages from Derek's manuscript. Still, he knows enough to have been sceptical when it was announced Richard would be coming to dinner. But Brad put his feelings aside the moment he realised who Richard was. Now it's all smiles, as Brad walks through to the kitchen to refill their wine glasses. He passes Alberta, who walks backwards through the flat and occasionally reaches down to feel the carpet. She pulls exaggerated expressions of concern and intrigue. She doesn't say anything to Brad, Derek or Richard, and they, in turn, choose not to acknowledge her.

"How's the book coming along?" Richard asks, but Derek isn't paying attention. He looks out the window, through which he can see a woman in the block of flats opposite. She stares right back at him, tears in her eyes.

"Bradley, come sit here." Richard pats the chair next to his as Brad returns, a glass in each hand and a third precariously balanced between the two. Brad takes the seat and Richard puts his arm around him. "I want to try something. Something I think will help Derek with his little book."

Alberta lies flat on the floor, passing one arm through the air, delicately picking out, examining, and sometimes eating pieces of nothing.

"Tell me, Bradley, have you ever told my sweetlittledarlingboy how you *really* feel?"

The sound of a passing fire truck is suddenly extinguished, and a silence fills the room, broken only by Alberta as she writhes across the carpet.

"I'm not sure what you mean." Brad says, awkwardly trying and failing to release himself from Richard's embrace.

"What I mean, Bradley, is that, in my experience, young couples are always keeping secrets. Don't get me wrong, it's rarely anything big. But, if you ask me, you should share *everything* with the one you love."

The more Derek looks at Richard the more he notices ways in which his father appears different compared to the image he had developed in the years they spent apart. His eyes are slightly brighter, his hair not as grey. It is only in these arbitrary details that Derek sees any change. In all the ways that matter, he is much the same. And he still wears that same smug smile.

"Well, I know Derek likes to keep himself to himself, but that's alright," Brad says. "As long as we get along fine. And we do, so—"

"Just fine?"

"We get along great."

"Is it fine or great?"

"Well—"

"So there's doubt?"

"No, no, no. Really, Richard, there's nothing even worth mentioning."

"Something not worth mentioning is still something."

Derek abruptly stands, as though the action alone would be enough to end this line of questioning. Alberta also stands, for reasons unknowable.

"Come on, Brad, sweetfuturesoninlawofmine. Just one thing. It will help to talk about it, I'm sure."

"Hey, Brad, why don't you show Richard that book you were telling me about. Brad's a big reader, like yourself. He has a spectacular collection of self-help books. I think you could get a lot out of them."

"Yes, I've just been reading *Be Yourself, Or Else*."

"Have you got anything that will help you talk about your feelings?"

"I *can* talk about my feelings."

"Mr Brad feels as though Mr Derek spends too much time moping." Alberta says, lighting a vogue and adjusting her sunglasses.

"Moping?"

"Wait, I never said that."

"You did not need to say. I saw it behind the door."

"Moping?"

"Since he lost his job, Mr Derek has not been the same."

"Fucking moping?"

Without warning or explanation. Alberta quickly leaves the flat, slamming the door behind her.

"How come you lost your job?"

"Moping? I can't believe what I'm hearing. Moping?"

"Maybe 'moping' isn't the right word. But you could say you've been holding on to your past."

"How about I hold on to your balls and tear them the fuck off, Brad? Then we can talk about my past you fucking fuckface fuck."

"You were in PR, right? What happened?"

"He got caught up in the whole fiasco with Top Notch."

"Hey, I love that guy!"

"Fuck you! You're both against me!"

"To be fair, Brad, it does sound like you're against him."

The door bursts open, and Alberta runs in, cigarette dangling from her lips and her hands full of raw meat, some of which falls to the floor. She ignores the spillage, and goes straight for the fridge, in which she starts methodically placing hunks of chicken and pork.

"What are you doing?"

"It's good meat. Your meat is bad meat. This is good meat."

"I didn't think the meal was bad." Richard says.

"Mr Richard, do you want to know something about me? I have never had an unhappy day in my life."

As Alberta places the last breast in the fridge, Brad excuses himself, grabs a half full bottle of wine from the counter, and locks himself in the bedroom. It's only in the ensuing calm that Derek realises just how drunk he is. His still-full plate of bad meat and vegetables is a reminder that he hasn't eaten all day. His eyes are drawn to the startling amount of empty wine bottles by the bin, and a new wave of nausea hits him. Still, Richard is fills yet another glass, and though Derek makes meek objections, the older man simply puts a a finger to his lips and slides the drink in Derek's direction. Though he feels he might be sick at any moment, he swallows it down, knowing full well that when the time comes he won't have the energy to make it to the kitchen sink, let alone the bathroom.

No further words are spoken between the two men. Richard pours glass after glass from a seemingly endless supply of bottles, while Derek, each time, holds his hand over the vessel and shakes his head. But Richard simply nods and the hand is withdrawn. Eventually there comes a point when Derek brings the glass to his lips, even as he shakes his head. Then he stops shaking all together until, inevitably, he throws up on the table, on his lap, a little by his feet, a lot on the bathroom floor and even more in the toilet. Twice he mistakes the redness of his vomit for blood, then realises it obviously isn't. But not before he throws up even more at the sight of it.

He dreams about Lena again. He saves her this time. It's just like a movie. He holds her in his arms. The building is behind them, in flames, but they don't look back. Then the credits roll, but the movie goes on. Lena goes back to her unhappy home. Her husband is cold and unloving. Her children are sick and dying. Her job is too hard and pays too little. She's always too hungry or too full or too hot or too cold and her legs and back always ache and her stomach always hurts and she has pains in her head and her neck and her feet and her hands and she's tired. She's so, so tired. And life is doing its dirty work on her in a way that death never would. And it's all Derek's fault.

An old lady taps Derek's shoulder as he's stood at a crossing in Barking. She's almost half his height, and has to squint from the sun when she looks up at him.

"You know, you look a lot like my grandson."

"Oh?"

"Yes. My grandson was killed. Just two days ago. Right there."

She points in the direction of some bushes at the other side of the road. There's a lamppost with a bouquet of flowers tied to it, still in their plastic wrapping.

"Just there. You see? Just there by those bushes. Over there. See?"

Derek nods.

"He was twenty three years old. Just there. By those bushes."

"I see."

"You see?"

A grey Astra comes round the corner and Derek prepares himself. But then the light turns red, the man turns green, and the old woman shuffles off toward the lamppost. As the Astra rolls out of view, the woman unties the flowers, removes the plastic, and shoves them, loose, in her handbag.

"Just here," she calls over to Derek. "Just here by these bushes." She stamps twice on the concrete. "Killed. He was twenty three years old."

This morning Derek miraculously failed to agitate the uncharacteristically calm commuters, though he moved painfully slow through the tube station, occasionally stopping to examine nothing in particular. The man whose bike he stepped out in front of managed to stop just in time and, for some reason, actually apologised. Three times he narrowly avoided falling bird shit.

Now he's stood at the lights, watching this woman take out a picture of her grandson and tape it to the lamppost. The man in the picture looks nothing like Derek. There are no more cars coming to take him away.

"Cuntish, isn't it?" The woman cries.

From somewhere nearby comes the sound of chanting. Derek follows it to find a demonstration happening outside a Polish mini-mart. A handful of grotesque men the colour of wafer-thin ham stand around, hunched and slack-jawed. They're dressed in too-tight Fred Perry polo shirts and milkshake-stained Harrington jackets. They chant, though not in unison. No two men say the exact same thing, though they occasionally land on the same word at the same time, 'country', 'home', 'English'. One man, who looks to be the oldest of the bunch, screams all the racial slurs he can think of at the top of his lungs, while a younger man beside him laughs nervously.

One man breaks off and walks towards Derek. By the time he realises it is Magnus, it's too late to turn away.

"I was hoping to see you here," he says. He wears a blue badge with a picture of a hand making the 'OK' gesture.

"Were you?"

"Yeah, I put that leaflet through your letterbox. Now I know what a Top Notch supporter you are, I thought we could even carpool together. You know, for any future events."

Derek notices a stack of placards lying on the ground by the shop. One reads, 'TOPS OFF FOR TOP NOTCH'.

"He's only round the corner if you fancied a catch up?"

Derek doesn't fancy a catch up, but he's already being guided away from the shop, down the street, through an alley, down another street, through another alley and into the infamous Oily Fork Cafe.

Top Notch is dressed much the same as his supporters. It suits him the best. He's as big, bald, and misshapen as the others, but his Fred Perry fits his frame, and his Harrington is unstained. He sits opposite Derek, with Magnus at his side. The landlord leans in close, as though awaiting instructions. A man is sat in the corner, who Derek recognises as the same old man from the Sadsac headquarters. He eats scrambled eggs and reads a new issue of *Tygodnik Przegląd*. On the cover is a picture of the old man himself, holding a book. Derek doesn't understand the title. Behind the counter is a large, sweaty man with an unlit fag hanging from his mouth and two more behind each ear. He seems friendly with Top Notch, and occasionally gives him a stained-toothed smile.

"I never said, Magnus, but me and Derek here have some history. Back when I got fired from BAE, this poor sod got caught up in it all."

"How so?"

"Do you want to tell him? No? I don't blame ya. It was a fuckin' travesty."

Top Notch has only one good eye that stays fixed at all times on Derek. The other wanders toward the old man with his magazine.

"That recording they got of me telling my joke actually came from a mic that Derek had on him. He made a statement after that lass got herself killed, but when he came off stage the mic was still on. If you think they were mad for giving me the sack, they did the same to soft lad here just for fuckin' laughing."

"You're 'avin me on!"

"After that I had it in my head that Derek wasn't Good Son material, just because when he was asked about it he made out the joke weren't even funny."

"It *was* very funny," Magnus says.

"I mean, obviously it was funny. But then you sent us all that cash."

"Which were right good of you."

When Derek moved from Barrow to Botany Bay, he thought he wouldn't have to hear about Top Notch and the Good Sons. But here they are, together again.

"Laughing at a joke is *not* a sackable offence," says Magnus.

"Right! No matter how blue!"

"Blue humour is a proud British tradition. Who do you think of when you think of the British comedy greats?"

"Bernard Manning! Chubby Brown!"

"I've actually just remembered," Derek says, rising from his seat, "I've got to go. I've, uh, got a meeting with my publisher."

Derek rushes out the Oily Fork and back through the alleys, toward the road where the old woman mourned the death of her grandson. But he can hear footsteps behind him, and a voice calls out 'hey' or 'wait' or perhaps something else entirely. Derek turns around to see the old man, the one who reads *Tygodnik Przegląd,* and he's holding a butter knife covered in egg and breadcrumbs.

"Is this funny?" He asks. "Is this a joke to you?"

Before Derek can answer, Top Notch and Magnus come darting around the corner and tackle the old man to the ground. He thrashes under Magnus, as the landlord holds him down and Top Notch kicks him in the ribs and in the face. He frantically slices the air with his knife, not managing to catch anyone or do any damage. A couple of passers-by stand and silently watch, but mostly they just keep walking. The two continue to beat the old man for what feels to Derek like a very long time before any sirens can be heard. When the police do turn up, the old man is covered in blood. He's still alive, though you wouldn't know it to look at him.

"Well, Rico, if I'm being honest. And I hope I can be honest. If I'm being honest, I think it's... excuse my language, but I think it's a ruddy disgrace!"

"I will. Excuse your language. Linda. Because. To be frank. And I hope I can be frank. I also think. It's. A. Ruddy. Disgrace. Next up. We've got Mo. From Leeds. What do you make of all this? Mo. From Leeds."

"Hey, Rico. I know I'm in the minority here, but I think Derek and Top Notch did the right thing. Sure, Kacper lost his daughter, but it doesn't give him the right to go stabbing good British people!"

"Well Mo. From Leeds. You *are* in the minority. And furthermore. You are. Clearly. An imbecile. Goodbye Mo. From Leeds."

Derek is laid on the sofa, facing the ceiling. He's been like this for four hours, and knows he'd happily stay four more. Brad and Alberta sit cross-legged on the floor across the room. They watch him while the radio plays in Alberta's apartment, turned way up so they can hear it from where they are.

Brad, filled with a sense of purpose and responsibility, stands up and takes Derek in his arms. He carries him like a baby, out of the

47

room. Alberta opens her eyes wide, which you'd see if it wasn't for her sunglasses.

Derek says nothing. He's a dead weight. He lets Brad carry him downstairs and out the building. He carries Derek all the way to the station, and all through the journey to the city. People double take and whisper and shake their heads.

As they pass a newly built DAS facility, Derek notices a billboard, advertising Kacper Symanski's book, *Goodbye Darling, Hello Sadness*. Not only that, he realises that people all around him are carrying copies of it. And they're all crying. There are people crying everywhere. Derek lets Brad put him down, and he stands up on his own. There are so many miserable faces, so many dead eyes and wet cheeks. He overhears someone say to a friend that people are throwing themselves from London Bridge. Derek has never heard such rave reviews. He turns to Brad and says, "You know, when I think about it, the joke was a bit funny."

But now Brad is crying too.

THE WONDERBOY TRILOGY

I. *Wonderboy Returns*

Brian Breedon sits in a reinforced wheelchair
that still barely holds his weight. He spent last
month bed-bound and bereft. His muscle has
turned to fat. The wheelchair once belonged to
Karl, the husband of his upstairs neighbour, a
frail old woman called Ingrid. She lost Karl to
the Sadness two weeks ago. He won't be
needing it anymore. The reinforcements were
applied by Arthur, Brian's brother-in-law, who
sits on a tree stump and reads a newspaper.
They left London this morning. Ingrid packed
them some sandwiches, but Arthur hates tuna
and he can't get Brian to eat solids. Brian saw
things in London that couldn't be unseen, and
he's been catatonic with malaise ever since.

Arthur finishes the paper and leaves it
on the stump. They're half way through their
mile-long journey across the dense woodland
between the parked car and Linda's cottage.
Arthur struggles to get the chair moving again.
It requires constant motion to keep it from
getting stuck. Before they can gain any
momentum, one of the wheels hits a rock and
the chair tips forward. Brian falls to the ground,
where he remains stiff, in a seated position.

Brian is unnaturally big, with a bulbous
head. His eyes are narrow and his brow

furrowed. Every now and then he cries out in pain.

Arthur trudges to Brian's side and tries to lift him out the dirt. He grabs him by the waist, the shoulders, by his shirt and his neck, attempts to drag him by his feet and turn him over but nothing works. Exhausted, he collapses and looks at his brother-in-law's mud-caked face. For a second it seems as though Brian is looking back at him, but when Arthur moves, Brian's eyes don't follow.

When Arthur finally succeeds in returning Brian to his chair, Brian whimpers, rolls his head from his right shoulder to his left and stares, unblinking, into the void.

Arthur opens the door to the cottage too abruptly, knocking a stack of *Judy For Girls* Annuals against the wall. He hits his head on the door as it recoils. He feels like collapsing in defeat right then and there. Any other day he would manoeuvre his way around, but he knows the clutter in the hall will make it impossible for the wheelchair. He stands at the entrance and decides what can be shifted. There's a rolled-up rug, purportedly from India, that hasn't been unrolled for decades. He moves it outside. There's a suit of armour, complete other than the helmet, which is replaced by a deflated football with a fez on top. He moves it outside. There's a four-foot Sarcophagus that bears an uncanny resemblance to the late Dale Winton, filled with VHS tapes. He moves it outside. He continues the process until there is enough room to get the wheelchair through the hallway, and the front of the house looks like a jumble sale.

Arthur never used to think of his father-in-law as a hoarder. The word, for him, conjured up images of filthy rooms filled with piles of old, damp books and rotting rubbish. He once viewed the bags of garishly colourful tat that the old man brought back from the nation's charity shops and boot sales as being delightfully kitsch. He used to like the thoughtlessly arranged displays. The disused fridge filled with garden gnomes, Sgt Pepper Pots from Liverpool lined up by the fireplace, Soviet era pin-badges tacked to door frames. Then his father-in-law died, and Linda inherited the cottage on the condition that she would keep everything safe. Now that Arthur has to live in the tat museum, he hates it.

In stark contrast to the rest of the house, the spare room is almost empty, other than a single bed. Arthur looks from Brian to bed to Brian, trying to figure out how to go about bringing the two together.

He tips the wheelchair, letting Brian fall onto the mattress, then hoists his feet up and straitens out his legs. He adjusts Brian's arms and his body until he looks relatively comfortable and puts the blanket over him.

Brian's tortured expression doesn't change throughout. He doesn't even flinch when the bed collapses under his weight and a jagged piece of wood cuts into his leg.

It takes Arthur another two hours to reinforce the bed. He uses awkwardly chopped pieces of wood from the stumps of trees behind the cottage. When he's done he jumps up and down on the bed to make sure it holds. Though unsightly, it's sturdy, and once again he goes through the process of getting Brian settled in. It sags under his weight, but doesn't collapse. Looking at Brian's sprawled, prone form, Arthur thinks about all the stories he's been told about his brother-in-law. They surely must be exaggerated.

Linda comes home late in the evening, bearing bags for life filled with food and fabric. She sees Arthur, laid on the settee, looking weak and weary. She only gives him a half-hearted, semi-sympathetic smile before dropping the bags and running into the spare room. She gasps at the sight of her brother. Arthur turns to see Linda in the doorway as she puts her hands on her hips and quickly accepts their situation. Once she does this it's as though nothing out of the ordinary has happened. She contentedly hums, waddles to her chair, sits, and drags the plastic table with the sewing machine towards her. She picks up an unfinished pair of Angel's wings that she's making for St Mary's year four Easter production and works on them, spending the rest of the night telling Arthur, in minute detail, about her exhausting day.

"They've closed the big Sainsbury's, you know? I had to go all the way to Morrison's. Their salad counter's better, though. So I guess there really are more reasons! Arthur? You see what I did there? I said, I guess there really are more reasons."

He stays silent throughout, occasionally picking newspapers off a regularly refilled pile he keeps by his legs.

Linda somehow manages to move Brian about with ease. She takes him in her arms, finding some hidden strength within herself. She puts him in his wheelchair in the morning and gracefully navigates routes through the tat-littered floor. She locks the chair in place at the dining table and uses the blender to make breakfast, laughing along at jokes cracked by Rambunctious Rico on the radio, turned up loud enough for her to hear over the whirr of the machine.

"Our Arthur did a good job of the bed, didn't he?" She says, spooning yogurt into Brian's mouth. "I told you about those films he used to make, didn't I? At dad's funeral? The stop-motion ones with the farmyard animals? Well he gave all that up. I thought they were funny too. Thing is, he says they're not supposed to be funny, Brian. He doesn't like talking about it, but I think a hobby would be good for him. All he does these days is shout at those newspapers. The other day he had a panic attack just *thinking* about global warming. I know, Brian, I worry about him too but he's a big boy, he can figure it out himself."

She leaves the dishes to soak in the sink and scurries back and forth through the house, finding pieces from their father's collection to show Brian. A bubblegum-pink phone shaped like a pair of lips, a figurine of Hitler bent over with a pin cushion for an arse, a frog smoking a cigar wearing a hat that says, 'Cuba'. She finds her signed print of Rambunctious Rico and the brief letter he wrote in response to the very lengthy letter she wrote. She shows off all the costumes she's made for St Mary's. Jesus' robes and wise men's crowns. She puts on different outfits she's made for herself. They are colourful and erratic. Crocheted leg warmers that come to her chest, flowing gowns with Pam Ayres stanzas stitched on the back, hats with green thread hanging down like hair extensions. She brings him all these things, making imagined conversation, sometimes doing her stunningly accurate impression of his voice, replying to her own questions. She thinks back to a time when they were children and she would tell him wild, made up stories about what she did at school and who she met in the woods and what she wanted to do when she grew up and he would smile enthusiastically and gasp and laugh and pick her up and move her through the air like she could fly and swing her around by her arms and dress her up in fancy dress costumes. She thinks about all this and tries hard not to cry. She succeeds, just about.

II. *Wonderboy Rises*

Linda insists on bringing Brian to the shop, despite Arthur's protests. The shop sits half way between their cottage and Upper Slaughter, the nearest village. It's called, 'The Sherborne Times', though no such newspaper has been published in more than 30 years, a fact that Arthur regularly points out. As well as the usual necessities, they sell a wide range of Osian O'Shea's home-brewed ales. Osian's wife, Stretch Arm Sandra works behind the counter. She has a long, pointed nose, long eyelashes, long white hair, a long chin, ear lobes that wildly flap on windy days, and breasts to her knees. She even speaks in long, drawn out sentences.

"You know those Barry boys from St Mary's came in yesterday and they took a whole load of Mars bars, they did, a whole load of Mars bars, if you can believe it, not just one or two, either, but a whole load of them, Linda, if you can fathom that, it was just off that counter over there, can you picture it? Can you see it with your mind's eye? Linda? Seven to nine of them, young boys, no older than ten, young boys, they were, stealing Mars bars, right off that counter over there, can you imagine?"

Osian carries boxes from the front of the shop to the back with Arthur's assistance. Osian is pug nosed and tiny-eyed. He's got stubby fingers, short legs, and small feet. The boxes are filled with novelty spy kits. Osian has a new hobby every month, and this is his latest. Walkie-talkies, night-vision goggles, dart traps, and trip wires. He intends to use them to play pranks on the kids from St Mary's, who come up on their bikes after school to buy bags of the special chewy sweets Sandra sells. They're actually just regular sweets that Sandra fills her hands with and squishes together when she's stressed.

Arthur goes through the newspapers, picking out one of each, while Osian shows Linda a tactical mirror from one of the boxes, collapsible for quick concealment in sticky situations. No one mentions Brian, who sits with his back to them, facing the ales. Sandra eyes up Fat Barry, one of the thieves from St Mary's, as he fills several paper bags up with sweets. He knows he's being watched, and smiles at Sandra as he pays. On his way out, he knocks into Brian's wheelchair. Brian lifts his head slightly to meet Fat Barry's gaze. The boy gasps and runs out the door.

As Linda wheels Brian out, bags hanging from the chair's handles, she sees Fat Barry half-hidden in some bushes across the road. He's with his friends, Lanky Barry, Specky Barry, Poor Barry, Barry-No-Daddy, and Joe. Poor Barry points to Brian, whose head is still bowed, and looks to Fat Barry for confirmation. Fat Barry nods his head, while Specky Barry and Barry-No-Daddy shake theirs. There is an air of general disagreement between the lot of them, but Linda can't make out what it is they are saying. Without really knowing why, she quickens her pace, leaving Arthur confused, unable to see what's going on past his stack of papers. He doesn't bother trying to catch up.

Even with the newspaper close to his face, Arthur knows Linda is looking at him from her chair, unsmiling and occasionally sighing. There's a particularly shocking image on the front page of a woman falling from the top of Big Ben, paired with an article about the recent Sadness outbreak in London. The woman in the picture wears sunglasses.

"You'd have thought she'd take them off." She says. "You don't want to get broken glass in your eyes."

When Arthur doesn't respond she turns the radio on. Rambunctious Rico is reporting live from the capital.

"The scenes. I'm seeing here. Are devastating. They're fishing dead bodies. Out the Thames. Parents are binding. Their children and tying. Them to their beds."

Arthur sighs, but doesn't look up.

"I spoke today. To an officer. From the metropolitan police. He shared a story. That shook me to my very core. Miss Emily Farley. Thought to be. One of the first victims of the Sadness. Was discovered. Nine weeks after her death. In her flat. In Southwark. When trying to contact her family. And friends. They were all. Found to have suffered. The same fate."

Even when Arthur has gone to bed, and the newspaper rests on the chair arm, Linda stares at the picture of the woman falling. It's half one in the morning when she starts on the sewing machine. She works quietly, quickly, and effortlessly, glancing at the newspaper every now and then. It takes almost all her material to make something big enough, patched together from different coloured fabric. She uses the little she has left to make a bandana for him to wear on his face. She's far from ashamed, but fears what people's reaction would be if they realised who Brian really was.

"It's unnecessary." Arthur says across the table at breakfast. "I say it's good if people recognise him. It'll get them to stop asking where he is. It's not as if he could do anything about what's going on anyway."

Linda ignores him and smiles at Brian in his new muumuu and mask. Brian wails and rocks his head from side to side.

The Barry boys see Brian again as Linda wheels him towards the Sherborne Times. This time when Poor Barry points him out, everyone seems to be in agreement that Fat Barry has it all wrong, and Joe goes back to complaining that Lanky Barry is taking more than his fair share of the sweets. They all leave when they realise Linda is looking back at them, except Fat Barry, who chews his special sweets and narrows his eyes with suspicion.

Osian has bought an old television, and intends to install CCTV cameras, so as to further his spying capabilities. The cameras haven't arrived yet, though, so he uses the TV to watch the news. After a segment on a young girl who got trampled at a Busboys concert, they run a piece on Wonderboy. The sound is down, so Linda can't hear what's being said, but a montage of footage, mostly recorded on witness' phones, shows him saving cats from trees and children from burning buildings, tackling muggers to the ground and helping old ladies cross the road. There's a video of him at Speakers Corner, and Linda imagines he's probably saying something about responsibility and kindness and love. In all these clips he wears his trademark suit. The red leotard, the blue pants, the yellow cape and the black mask. The orange Crocs he wore for comfort's sake.

"It's a shame, ain't it?" Osian says to no one in particular.

"This a friend of yours?" Asks Stretch Arm Sandra, nodding toward Brian, finally acknowledging his presence.

"He's my brother. He's staying with us for a while."

Osian turns around and looks at Linda sympathetically.

"He's not got it, has he? The Sadness?"

Linda nods.

"Poor fella."

Before she leaves, Linda buys herself a bag of Sandra's sweets and, uncharacteristically, a bottle of Osian's ale.

Arthur watches his wife from behind his paper as she takes small, quick sips of Osian's National Splendour. He says nothing about the drinking, but registers it as unsettling. Brian is positioned between them and, unseen, he looks from Arthur to Linda to Arthur to Linda.

Again, Linda waits until Arthur goes to bed before returning to the sewing machine. She is already drunk, but still works silently and mechanically, knowing exactly what to do without even having to think about it. She remembers how it's done. She made the very first. The leotard, the pants, the cape, the mask. She even knows where her father stored his collection of hideous Crocs.

In the early hours of the morning, Linda dresses Brian, knowing she won't have long before Arthur gets up. She wheels Brian out into the woods, bringing the paper with the picture of the falling woman. She sits Brian on a tree stump and puts the paper in his hands. She manipulates his stiff body so he looks natural, crossing one leg over the other. She puts make up on him and slicks his dark hair back. Through his mask, his narrowed eyes seem to reflect concentration more than anguish. He occasionally shrieks, but Linda waits for it to pass before taking the pictures with her father's *Hello Kitty* Instax camera.

By the time she hears Arthur moving in the bedroom, she has already hidden the suit in a kitchen drawer and returned the newspaper to the chair arm. Brian is in his muumuu once more, but Linda leaves the mask on as long as she can before Arthur comes out. She takes a moment to look at him and imagine he is still the same old Wonderboy.

"I'm glad to see you're enjoying the fruit of my labour." Osian says as Linda moves several bottles of ale from the shelf to the counter, on which Fat Barry is sat, swinging his legs, bags of sweets stuffed into every one of his blazer pockets. His eyes move back and forth, following Linda's movements.

"Where's your brother?" He asks.

"He's back at the house with Arthur."

"You know who I think he looks like?"

Linda looks up at the TV, ignoring the question. An Asian woman in a suit is rustling some papers. Behind her is a graphic of a priest with his trousers around his ankles, arms raised, as if to say, 'I didn't do it.' The image disappears, replaced by one of Wonderboy. Fat Barry notices this and jumps down from the counter.

"Can you turn this up, Stretch... I mean, Mrs. Sandra?"

Sandra rolls her eyes and reaches for the remote.

"A picture showing London's most beloved eccentric, Wonderboy, surfaced yesterday."

The picture of Brian sat on the tree stump appears on screen and Fat Barry is stunned.

"Wonderboy was thought to be missing. Many guessed he was another victim of the mysterious case of mass hysteria that is still sweeping the capital. The sociogenic illness, known colloquially as, Sadness, has caused tens of thousands of people all across the city to fall into severe bouts of depression and panic."

"Well there you go, Fatty Bazza, he's right as rain." Osian says.

Fat Barry's smile fades. He climbs back up on the counter to get a closer look at the picture on screen. He squints at it until it disappears, then jumps back down and walks straight out the shop, a few sweets falling through holes in his inside pockets as he does.

When Linda gets home, Arthur is waiting in the living room, pacing back and forth with a newspaper in hand. He holds it open for her to see the picture of Brian.

"Well, I think it worked." She says.

Fat Barry starts hiding in the bushes by Linda and Arthur's cottage. He uses Osian's spy equipment, now that the shop owner has moved on to a new hobby, CB radio. The boy holds binoculars to his face with one hand and dips into his paper bag of sweets with the other. He sits in the same spot every day between school and supper time. Arthur tries to shoo him away on multiple occasions, but every time he approaches, Fat Barry goes completely still and pretends to be invisible until Arthur gives up and goes back inside.

Linda gets drunk on Osian's Razor every evening and has long one-way conversations with her brother about all the amazing things he did as Wonderboy. Brian stops crying out in pain as much. Instead he thrashes his head from side to side and occasionally kicks one leg out.

It takes Linda a week of adjusting and perfecting her plan to convince Arthur to help her pull it off. For the first couple of days she gets a firm 'no'. Then he stops saying anything and just wearily shakes his head. Eventually, he gives up. He goes to the cupboard he hasn't opened in over a year and takes out his stands and lights and lenses and cameras. He spends the night trying to remember how everything works, his brain fried and scrambled by months of reading bad news.

They work during school hours, so as to be sure that Fat Barry will be none the wiser. Linda wheels Brian while Arthur carries his equipment. They hang a green sheet between two trees and stand Brian up straight so he stiffens, statuesque in front of it. Even at the remarkably fast pace that Arthur is able to work at, the process takes hours, moving Brian by increments, repositioning him whenever he jolts or shakes his head around. Arthur directs Linda, showing her what needs to go where. They take thousands of pictures, adjusting his arms and mouth, not stopping until they know Fat Barry will be leaving school.

In the evening, Arthur and Linda share a bottle of Osian's Razor, while he edits the pictures together, making it appear as seamless and realistic as possible. He adds filters to reduce the quality, masking the imperfections. They use a voice recording Linda had made the night before, impersonating her brother, reciting a two minute speech filled with Brian's trademark humour and heartfelt sincerity.

They upload it to YouTube under the name, 'Wonderboy Returns', and by the morning, 500,000 people have watched it.

III. *Wonderboy Forever*

"A real inspiration. Wonderboy. Until recently. Thought to be lost. Like so many others. In the capital."

Arthur reads about a sex scandal involving the US President and a teenage girl from a K-Pop group. Linda doesn't drink for the first night in weeks. She listens to Rambunctious Rico, chin rested on her folded arms, filled with a great amount of pride in her achievement. They haven't seen Fat Barry all day.

"In. The video. We see Wonderboy. Talking. Just like he did at Speakers Corner. About unity. About friendship. About brotherhood. About responsibility."

The views on 'Wonderboy Returns' increase at an alarming rate, and Rambunctious Rico seems to be revitalised by the first piece of good news he's had the chance to report on in a long time.

Arthur is content for it to end there, but Linda isn't.

"Won't it seem suspicious if he suddenly vanishes again?" she asks. "What about everything he said?"

"I think you're forgetting, Linda, that he didn't actually say anything."

"He can't just give them all this hope and comfort and then disappear off the face of the earth. Look how happy he's made everyone."

"It says here that the number of Sadness cases in London is approaching a million."

"Maybe more videos will help somehow."

"I doubt it."

"It helps me. It helps Brian."

Though Arthur is sceptical about whether this is true, he finds it hard to deny.

Brian has been acting differently in small but noticeable ways. He doesn't yelp, moan, or cry out as much as he used to. Instead of violently kicking his legs, he's started fidgeting. He twists his feet around and knocks them together. He's stopped shaking his head from side to side, and has started stretching his neck out, as if reaching for something.

When Linda comes home with several bottles of Osian's Razor, Arthur finally submits. They dress Brian up and wheel him back out to the woods. It becomes a daily routine. They make new, increasingly elaborate videos. Some with Brian sat on a tree stump, providing comforting commentary on the latest news stories, some where he smokes a pipe and talks about how to care for people with the Sadness, one where he gives a yoga tutorial. Each time they record Linda's approximated speeches, imagining what Wonderboy would say. Arthur works out how to move Brian's mouth to make the words match.

Arthur's stack of papers piles higher and higher, as the miserable news goes unread. He finds himself becoming restless. His dreams are filled with awful, impossible things. The devil comes to Upper Slaughter, slaughters all the children of St Mary's, black clouds of smoke cover the land, block out the sun, filth filled lakes drown in nuclear waste, animals turn inside out, sheep with twelve eyes walk on their hind legs, men in dark suits take people away from their loved ones. He wakes up in the middle of the night, sweating profusely and gasping for breath. He gets drunk on Osian's Razor through the day and the stop-motion films of Brian's sermons become increasingly lackluster and jittery. It doesn't go unnoticed. People in the comments start asking whether Wonderboy has Parkinson's.

"We've got to step it up a bit, Arthur." Linda says as they wheel Brian though the woods. "We don't want to find Fatty Baz in the bushes again."

Arthur suddenly stops in his tracks. Linda doesn't notice right away, still scrolling through comments for their video, 'Modern Malaise: The Wonderboy Perspective'. Brian shuffles in his chair, stretches his neck, and coughs. Linda, hearing this, turns around.

"Arthur? What's up?"

He stands there, staring back at her. His fists are clenched.

"Are you worried about the comments? Because it'll be alright, you know? We just need to put a bit more time into this one."

"I'm not doing it." He says.

"What do you mean you're not doing it?"

"I'm done. This isn't my problem, Linda. I'm not doing it anymore."

He pushes Brian towards her and storms off to the cottage, where he stacks two piles of newspapers, picks them up, and retreats to the spare bedroom. By the time Linda makes it back he's locked the door from the inside and adamantly refuses to leave. All Linda can hear is loud tuts and heavy sighs and frustrated groans and occasional weeping as Arthur reads and reads and reads about scams and schemes and scandals, greedy billionaires and starving single mothers and cheating husbands and uncontrollable youths, homelessness and poverty and war and terrorism, editorials and gossip columns and lonely hearts columns and sports sections and advertisements for second hand sofas and local news and national news and international news, headlines and subheadlines and bylines and datelines, editor's letters, readers' letters, open letters, and endless, hopeless, abject misery and pain and hurt and grief and suffering and despair.

Now Brian sleeps in Linda's bed, and Linda sleeps on the floor.

"Wonderboy. Whose YouTube channel. 'WonderboyForever'. Has over. Ten million subscribers. Has inexplicably. Gone silent."

Linda drinks her third Osian's Razor of the morning, turns off the radio and stumbles into her bedroom.

"Time to get up. Brian. Come on. We've got work to do." She shakes her brother, though he's already awake. "Brian. Brian, come on. Wonderboy to the rescue."

She clumsily dresses him in his unwashed suit and drops him into his wheelchair. On the way out she bangs on the door to the spare room.

"Last chance to help, Arthur. We're gonna do it with or without you."

"It says here that people are starting to think Wonderboy has got the Sadness." He yells from the still locked bedroom.

"You haven't got the Sadness have you, Brian? *No Linda, I'm right as rain, Linda. Let's go help people, Linda. Screw you Arthur, you miserable bastard.* You hear that, Arthur? He says screw you."

"It says here..."

"Oh, piss off."

Linda gasps for breath as she pushes the wheelchair uphill to get to the clearing. The ground is wet from last night's rain, and she is unsteady on her feet. The wheels of the chair get stuck in the mud whenever she stops to take a breath. At one point the chair tips forward and Brian almost falls out, but she grabs him just in time.

Every time she pins one side of the green backdrop to a tree, the other side falls off, so she trudges back and forth, sighing and wheezing. She notices how much weight Brian has lost since he first came, and though it makes it easier to get him out the chair, it also makes it harder to get him to stay stood up. He's become weak and fragile. She finally manages it. He stands in his costume, dirty and damp, occasionally stretching his neck out, but mostly holding his head low. She wipes sweat from her brow and looks at him. She feels a lump in her throat and almost breaks down then and there. She only snaps out of it when she hears a branch break behind her and turns to see Fat Barry, mouth full of sweets and tears in his eyes. She forgot to bring the camera, anyway.

Children gather outside the cottage. All the Barrys, along with several other St Mary's students. Linda has locked herself in. She calls through for Arthur but he rarely responds. If he does, it's just to report what the papers say.

"It says here that they've worked out the whole Wonderboy scam."

She blends revolting concoctions out of the few items they have left in the kitchen to feed to Brian. He doesn't complain. She lives off her Osian's Razor supply, terrified to confront the curious crowd.

She sits cross-legged on the living room floor, repairing a broken angel's wing that had been tossed aside long ago. She looks up to see Brian is staring back at her. She moves to the left, then to the right, and his eyes follow. He rearranges himself in his seat, coughs, and stretches his neck out.

"You know what I was thinking about, Brian? *What's that Linda?* I was thinking about that Superman film we used to watch. *Quest For Peace?* That's the one. You know, I saw it on TV again the other day. It was just awful. *But we loved it, Linda.* Yeah, we did, didn't we? Remember, we used to talk about what superpowers we would want? *And you learned how to sew so you could make us costumes.* Yeah. Those were good times."

Brian coughs again. He twists his neck more frantically. He struggles and pants and yelps and moans and kicks his legs out. Linda tries to get up to help him but when she gets close he kicks her. She loses her balance and stumbles backwards. As she does, he suddenly rises out his chair. He stops coughing and starts screaming. He's screaming louder than Linda has ever heard anyone scream, and he does it over and over and over until he starts to croak and lose his voice. Then he collapses to the floor and thrashes like he's having a seizure. He wretches and stretches his neck out like he's trying to get his head to detach itself. Linda crawls towards him and strokes his hair.

After a while he calms down. His breathing become measured and steady as Linda wraps him in a blanket and holds him to her body by the warmth of the fire. They stay like this for hours.

In the early hours of the morning she goes searching for the last bottle of Osian's Razor. On her way back from the kitchen she gently knocks on the guest room door, but Arthur only grumbles and groans.

When she returns to Brian she realises something is wrong. He's pale. His eyes are narrower than ever before. He doesn't breathe. Linda looks at his prone form and feels a sensation through her body like she's falling from a great height. She thinks about the woman from the newspaper. Thinks of her at the base of Big Ben with broken glass in her eyes.

She feels like she's losing her legs as she slowly walks toward the spare room. She taps on the door, then knocks, then bangs, then, somewhere between weeping and screaming, throws herself against it, breaking it down.

Arthur is laid on the bed, bereft, catatonic with malaise, eyes narrow, brow furrowed. Every now and then he cries out in pain.

VANISHING ACT

In the early hours of Saturday morning, Kurt stares out the kitchen window of his ground floor flat at the ginger kid across the road. The kid, who Kurt thinks must be around seven, is pale and angular, with the vacant eyes of a serial killer. He teases the family cat, pointing the red light of a laser pen onto the passenger side door of his father's car. The cat claws at the dot until the scratches run deep. When the kid grows bored, he turns off the light and runs inside. When the dot disappears the cat freezes, staring at his handiwork with a haunted expression.

On the radio, some feel-good pop song plays. A woman sings about loving yourself no matter how much the haters try to bring you down. But just as Kurt cracks his solitary egg, and the singer describes herself as 'curvaceous and outrageous', the music abruptly cuts out. The sudden silence gives Kurt an unsettling sense of déjà vu. The feeling doesn't last long, however, as everyone's favourite DJ, Rambunctious Rico, resumes his trademark disjointed patter.

"Sorry. Everyone, we seem. To have encountered some. Technical difficulties. That was. Wait, who was that? Anyway, now. We have. The Busboys with. 'Cleaning The Table Of Love'."

Kurt eats his egg and doesn't sing along. He's lost all joy in musical participation, though he knows not when. There was a time he would spend hours aimlessly wandering the streets performing one-man renditions of whole albums from memory. At some point, though, just the thought of whistling or humming began to make him feel queasy. So now he sits in silence, with the absent look of someone who's forgotten the lyrics.

After the 'hot tracks', Rambunctious Rico moves on to the 'hot takes', fielding a call from some bewildered sounding woman from Slough.

"Whatever happened to having a 'stiff upper lip', eh? Am I the crazy one for thinking about the families? Am I, Rico? Am I Crazy? Should they kart me off with the doolallies just because I think the DAS should take a moment to think about the poor mothers? Should they? Rico? Should they kart me off?"

Kurt takes the 75 bus, seating himself behind two well-dressed pensioners who talk too loudly about their sons.

"Well my Gary, he's been transferred to that new place on Park Road. He's taken on a lot more responsibility but, oh, he works so hard, my Garry."

"Well my Barry, he was working with the DAS but he's moved up to one of those private centres just recently. He's earning more but it brings him down ever so much, you know? He comes home and..."

"Living with you, is he?"

"He is, Karen. It's a strain at times, you know?"

"Oh, yes Sharon, I imagine it is a strain at times."

"It is. It is a strain at times. But it's a joy at times too, you know?"

"Oh, well of course I imagine it is a joy. At times."

Kurt's phone vibrates in his pocket and he knows instinctively that it's his father. He lets it go to voicemail, a habit he has slipped into over the past couple of weeks without really knowing why. He's even been convincing himself that he's too busy to go over on Sundays, though he's unsure what it is he was supposed to be busy doing.

The bus makes a pained sound as it stops and a relieved sigh when the doors open. Kurt watches as one man gets on and no one gets off. Kurt finds it hard to place the man's age. In the face, he looks not too dissimilar to the ginger kid from across the street, but he wears the suit of a much older, taller, and fatter man. He repeatedly rolls his sleeves up and trips on his trousers. He seems fragile and the jolting of the bus as it moves away rattles him here and there. He clumsily makes his way toward the pensioners.

"Excuse me, ladies, would either of you be able to tell me the time?"

"It's a quarter to ten." Sharon says, looking at her watch.

"Exactly?"

She holds the watch closer to her face and squints. "Yes, exactly."

"Are you sure? How sure are you that it's a quarter to ten?"

She looks again, bringing the watch closer still, almost pushing it into her eye. "I'm not very sure, you know?"

The man-child arrogantly smiles. "Your eyesight isn't quite what it used to be, yes?"

The confusing nature of the exchange leaves Sharon slightly dazed and she says nothing.

"Well that's..." The man-child finds himself suddenly cut short as the bus turns and he is thrown to the floor. He struggles to get back up but no one assists him. Eventually he succeeds on his own, clutching the nearest pole with both hands. "That's a shame," he says to no one in particular. Then, looking back at Sharon, "But, uh, that's just a crying shame. Right. OK. Thanks."

The man-child turns and moves between poles toward the stairs. On the CCTV monitor, Kurt sees him tentatively make his way to the top deck. He sits down, puts his head in his hands, then slaps himself several times around the face.

"Karen, what were we talking about just now?"

"We were talking about my Gary. He's been transferred to that new place on Park Road, you know?"

"Oh, yes, I always wished I'd had a boy like your Gary."

Kurt sits in an unfamiliar room. He's heard on the news that all across the nation they're moving these groups to smaller buildings, since they are prone to becoming suicide hotspots. Kurt only started his course last week. They were still at Crown Place, which was several stories high. The ground around it had become dark with partially cleaned stains.

Someone has printed out hundreds of pictures and they adorn almost every inch of the walls. Curious puppies, adorable kittens, families smiling in green fields, children playing in sunny parks, beaches drenched in light. The printer had clearly started to run out of ink at some point. A few of the sunny parks are grayscale and some of the children's smiles seem faded.

Marcel, the group leader, sits at the front of the room, reclining in a way that pushes his plastic chair to its limit. His legs are spread wider than should be possible and you can tell, even seated, that he is unnaturally tall. His head, on the other hand, is particularly small and almost perfectly round, which is accented by the way he ties his red hair back into a tight ponytail.

"We have biscuits in the back, if anyone wants any." He says in a slow whisper.

Kurt wants the biscuits. So do most of the attendees, but no one moves.

Quiet Frank arrives late. Frank is a fat man who doesn't suit his size. He fills out spaces that seem like they'd be better left unfilled. His face is fixed in its usual expression of sheer terror. He grabs three biscuits and eats them whole before his arse hits either of the seats it takes up. Kurt wouldn't have found Frank's silence as noteworthy, had Boney Babs not leant in last week to point out that he hasn't spoken a word since he started the course, almost a year ago. This would be Quiet Frank's final session with the DAS 'Lifechangers' support group and, though attendance is mandatory, contribution is not, a loophole Frank seems to have taken full advantage of.

There's enough space in this new room for double the turnout. Everyone has taken care not to sit next to anyone else, creating a scatter graph of misery. There's Deirdre with the dying mother, Big Bertha with the backwards boy, a man known only as Plug who, on the surface, seems perfectly content, but every now and then goes dead-eyed for hours. Sometimes he seems one piece of bad news away from taking a romantic bath with a toaster.

"How have you been, Bertha?" Marcel asks, leaning back even further in his char, which cries for help.

"He's just a little boy!" She cries out, instantly bursting into tears. "How could they do that to a little boy?"

Like many people across the country who sign up for DAS services, Kurt made his decision based on a strange, uncharacteristically morbid impulse. Kurt has made it to his second week. It's not uncommon for people to grow so impatient that they end up doing the job themselves. Otherwise, they realise that whatever it was that they were under, they would be able to get over. Quiet Frank has been attending the sessions longer than anyone else here and, though he is near impossible to read, Kurt takes this as a sign that he is someone who likes to do things the right way.

"Have you got anything to say about that, Frank?" Marcel asks, at this point as close to being perfectly horizontal as he can possibly get.

Quiet Frank remains silent, looking straight through the reclining counsellor. Marcel sighs deeply in an act of unashamed unprofessionalism, and turns his attention to Kurt.

"What about yourself, Kurt, is it?"

Kurt shifts uncomfortably in his seat

"Yes. Oh. Uh. Well. It's kinda like. You know..."

Just as beads of sweat begin to appear on Kurt's forehead, Quiet Frank becomes abruptly alert. His horrified expression vanishes and a sense of deep calm comes over him as though, this past year, he has been daydreaming and now he is snapping out of it.

"It's just so strange, you know," he says, "one day you're yourself, you know? You're waking up, going to work, you know, just doing what you do. Not thinking about much, you know how it is? Not depressed, not nothing. Just living your life, you know? Then it's just like, woah. You know? This is it. This is all there is to it, you know? You're not just doing this for the shits and giggles. This isn't just a temporary thing, you know? This is it. This is all there is to it, you know? And, at the end of the day, what are you playing at? D'ya know? D'ya? 'Cos I don't. Then you start to wonder why you were ever alright, you know? You start to question yourself. Wasn't I feeling alright just a minute ago? Where did all this come from?

It's like the rug's been pulled from under you, you know? Suddenly you find yourself not wanting to get up. Not wanting to go to work, you know, 'cos what's the point? You know? What's the point? Well? What's the fucking point?"

Everyone in the room stares at Frank. Even after he's finished speaking, and his expression reverts to its former horror. The pained silence fills the room and weighs heavy on all in attendance. Kurt is especially struck by the whole thing, quietly impressed at how accurate Frank's prognosis seemed. He looks around and wonders whether everyone else feels the same, thinking he might take some comfort from the idea that, though he feels miserably alone, his misery and loneliness, at least, is not unique.

"That guy's not right in the head." Big Bertha says, shovelling several Sertraline into her mouth as Marcel's chair finally snaps, causing him to dramatically fall backwards, arse over head, limbs wildly flailing.

After two hours of counselling, half of the group members walk to the bus stop, and the other half to The Solemn Mule. Kurt feels as though these people, like himself, are creatures of habit. They stand in their same respective spots in the beer garden, acting as though they don't know each other. Kurt spots Marcel approaching, pint in one hand, vape pen in the other, his ponytail bobbing with each step. The other group members quickly stub out their fags, grab their drinks, and walk inside, heads low.

"So this is where the cool kids hang out?"

Kurt makes a pathetic attempt at a chuckle, though all he is able to muster is a near inaudible expulsion of air. Marcel doesn't seem to acknowledge any awkwardness as he sucks at his vape, letting cherry scented billows release in short bursts as he speaks. Kurt takes a particularly large swig of his pint before mustering the effort to contribute to the conversation. When he does speak, it comes out as though each individual word is a question. Like he's unsure about what he's doing, desperately searching for some sign of approval, some assurance that these are normal sounds to be making.

"So? How? Long? Have? You? Been? Doing? This? For?"

"Lifechangers? Oh, about two years now."

Kurt wants to ask if it's a rewarding line of work, but thinks too long about it, forming the words and structuring the sentence, not wanting to seem like someone who's only pretending to be human.

"It was my dad who got me into it."
Marcel says. "He works for Dignity. You know,
the private clinic?"

"Private?" Kurt asks, thinking it best to
stick to one word at a time.

"It's crazy what they do for you when
there's a bit of money involved. Double the
contact hours through the cooling-off period,
one-on-one counselling, real life affirming shit.
They even have this special package where
they erase all evidence that you ever even
existed. Saves your loved ones from getting all
down about it. Costs a fortune, though."

"I bet." Kurt says, considering the fact
that he can't afford to be forgotten.

As he walks back through the Solemn
Mule, Kurt sees the man-child from the bus
again, his face still red from the self-inflicted
slaps, and redder still from frustration as he
kicks a jukebox. Kurt briefly stops, trying to
remember the name of the song that's playing.
But he can't make it out as it skips and
becomes increasingly drowned out by the
attacks. Eventually the song cuts out all
together and the man-child smiles wide, filled
with serenity. He doesn't even resist as the
barman drags his limp body out the pub.

When he arrives back at his flat, Kurt goes
straight into a storage cupboard. He knows
what he's looking for, and he knows how to get

to it. The black A4 folder is inside a cardboard box, inside another cardboard box, under a Henry Hoover which is, in turn, covered by a patchwork blanket made by his late mother. The photos in the folder aren't a secret. They had simply been neglected. Kurt wonders if this is something the people at Dignity would have to find. If they really wanted to erase all evidence that he ever existed, how would they know how to get their hands on photos like these? Could they sniff them out? Could they see through doors? Through Henry? Or would they just burn the whole flat to the ground? What would happen to the Patels on the second floor?

Looking through the pictures that record his life from ages four through twenty, Kurt finds himself unable to feel any particularly strong emotions about the people he has known. His uncles, aunts, his mum, his stepmum, her daughter, his friends. He can't remember the last time he really considered what he thinks of the people he has surrounded himself with, or been surrounded by. They are just there. When he tries to push himself for an actual opinion on any one of these people, he realises he has none.

As he leafs back and forth, he finds himself repeatedly returning to one particular picture. In it, he is smiling more than he has ever known himself to smile. His arm is draped around a man who he doesn't recognise. Strangely, he wears a t-shirt with the same man's face printed on. Kurt can't get his head around this picture. He sits inside the cupboard, cross-legged, staring at the image until it gets to the point where he can't really see it anymore.

Kurt feels as though he has little to no control over his movements. He finds himself blindly walking into situations, without thinking about how he will handle them. In the week before he first went to the Department of Assisted Suicide, he was struggling to get out of bed. He hadn't initially thought of himself as being depressed, just confused. He once spent several hours thinking about going to the park. But what would he do when he got there? That's when he made the conscious decision to stop making conscious decisions. He would leave the flat and end up wherever he happened to end up. The first time he tried this, he ended up at the old DAS centre. This time he ends up at his childhood home.

   He is surrounded on all sides by the lavish houses of the rich. His family is not rich. The house, which slouches and sags, dark and decrepit, has been lived in by his relatives for generations. They stubbornly refuse to move. Kurt stands at the front door, unmoving, unfeeling, unthinking, waiting for his body to tell him what to do. He knocks.

"Who is it?" His stepmum calls out. Kurt tries not to react, aware that Martha is most likely watching him through the peephole, and knows full well who it is. The doormat reads 'All Are Welcome', a statement Kurt knows couldn't be further from the truth. He says his own name, which doesn't sound right to him and for a moment he wonders if he got it wrong. Martha opens the door an inch. She is dressed in clothes that could be mistaken as being more expensive than they are.

"You'll have to wait a moment while I change into something. I wasn't expecting guests."

Before Kurt can say anything, the door shuts and Martha retreats into the house for almost fifteen minutes. When she returns, she has a new pair of shoes and a rosary around her neck. She tells Kurt he must take his own shoes off, even though he is already in the process of doing so.

The inside of the house isn't nearly as gloomy as its exterior would suggest, though there is little decoration other than religious paraphernalia. There are multiple crosses of different shapes and sizes in each room, garish 3D prints of the Stations of the Cross, statuettes of obscure saints. His father has a strict rule about having no family portraits displayed, which he tells Martha is down to him being staunchly unsentimental. He has privately told Kurt, however, that it's because he finds Martha's daughter, Sarah, hideously ugly, and can't bear the thought of looking at her on a day to day basis.

Martha leads Kurt through to the kitchen, deeming every other room unsuitable for hosting purposes, again bringing up the fact that she wasn't expecting anyone. Martha is never expecting anyone.

Kurt sits on a dining room chair, but Martha remains standing, looking down at him, half smiling, unfazed by the awkward silence. She is known for her false politeness, as much as she is for her very real impertinence behind closed doors. Still, she can't help but look at Kurt as though he were an unwanted salesman, having to deliver his reasons for turning up at her door in the form of a pitch.

"Where's dad?"

"Oh, he's just popped to the shops."

"Sorry, I can come back some other time."

Martha shakes her head, but doesn't explicitly say that she would be opposed to the idea.

Kurt's childhood bedroom has hardly changed since he moved out ten years ago. There's a single bed adorned with black sheets that are still regularly washed, a record player that Kurt knows to be broken, and posters of bands Kurt is embarrassed to have ever liked. There are a few spaces where posters have been removed and only Blu Tack remains.

"Did something need to come down?"

"Oh, I wouldn't know anything about that, now. I never come in here."

Kurt notices a cross has been placed on his bedside table.

Kurt's dad returns, holding a set of keys close to his chest. He places them in a box marked 'keys' by the door and repeats the phrase 'they're in the key box' several times. When Kurt comes downstairs, Adrian smiles wide, opens his arms, and begins his ritualistic criticisms.

"You look like you need a shave; can I give you a shave? You want me to sort that for you? I've got some clothes off Harry Harryman, do you want them? They don't fit me, c'mon, take them! That shower of yours still not working? Because that's what it seems like, d'ya know what I'm saying? I'm being subtle, but you know what I'm saying, right? You can have one while you're here you know?"

Adrian is only 4'11". He excitedly circles his son, looking like a mouse taunting a cat. He offers Kurt food, which he declines, and tea, which he accepts.

In the living room, Martha puts the radio on as she darts around, moving items from one place to another, giving the illusion that she is tidying. Adrian sits on his tall, narrow chair, preferring nothing than to exist quietly, keeping his thoughts to himself. This is what Kurt imagines Adrian is doing, though he has no hard evidence to suggest that his father thinks much about anything. Softly, in the background, Rambunctious Rico talks through the radio.

"We're. Talking again about. The DAS. Caller. State your name. And location."

"Melvin from Doncaster."

"Melvin. From Doncaster. The Department of Assisted Suicide. Good? Or Bad?

"Good."

"Melvin. From Doncaster. Thinks the Department of. Assisted suicide is. Good. Thank you Melvin. From Doncaster."

Martha tuts as she moves a picture of 'Jesus falling for the second time' a fraction to the right.

"Whatever happened to a 'stiff upper lip'?" Asks Brenda from Slough. "Am I crazy for thinking about the families? Do they ever take a moment to think about the poor mothers?"

"I can't imagine my Sara ever going to one of those places." Martha says.

The mention of his stepdaughter causes Adrian to sit upright and shudder.

"Or yourself, for that matter, Kurt. What do you make of it? I know you can be a bit moody, but just abandoning all of your family and friends like that. Can you imagine it?"

Kurt looks to his father, but he isn't paying attention. Martha waits for a response, her feather duster half way between 'Jesus is nailed to the cross' and 'Jesus dies on the cross'.

"I best be getting off."

Adrian becomes alert and loses his smile before offering Kurt a lift. Martha's duster remains in her raised right hand and doesn't move until they've both left the house.

The car whirrs and splutters as it moves through winding roads. The CD player doesn't work, but the radio does.

"Tomorrow. We'll be taking calls from. All you Londoners. Hearing your concerns about. Brian Breedon. Where has our Wonderboy gone?"

Adrian doesn't take his eyes off the road. Kurt watches the reflection of his father through the passenger window, occasionally adjusting his focus to look at what they are driving past. He struggles to catch anything. It's dark now and the route between Adrian's house and Kurt's flat is mostly open fields with sporadic cottages. Kurt hears the sound of laughter from somewhere in the darkness, even though his window is closed. He wonders, not for the first time, if he is losing his mind.

"I got this off Toby Groper." Adrian says, the sudden sound of his voice startling Kurt.

"The car. Toby Groper sold it to me. Only took me a day to lose the keys. You know what I'm like. But this time I really couldn't find them. I'm talking about a whole week looking for these keys. Martha and I looked all over the house. I looked everywhere in the office. I retraced my steps. I was asking people I hardly knew if they'd seen a set of keys anywhere, y'know, describing them."

"Where were they?"

"Well, that's the thing. I can't even remember where it was I found them. I'm worried I'll lose them again and they'll end up in the same place. You're not like that. You're like your mum. You know exactly where everything's at. Even if you've never seen something before, you instinctively know where it could be found."

Kurt doesn't know if this is really the case or if his father is just fabricating an observation for the hell of it.

"You're very aware of what's going on around you. You've got stuff figured out."

Kurt feels a strange sense of familiarity and reassurance, though he knows not where it has come from. He listens to the music on the car radio and the feeling grows stronger. He can tell his father feels it too. Adrian scrunches his face trying to put a name to the song. Though Kurt doesn't feel like he really knows it, he finds the lyrics forming in his head before they have been sung. He instinctively places the phrases one after another, down to the singer's intonations and the musical flourishes.

An image comes into focus in his mind; his arm is draped around a man, his t-shirt has the man's face on it. It all comes to the surface. It all becomes as clear as Quiet Frank's epiphany.

Then they see a broken down car in the road ahead. It would be easy to miss in the darkness, but the driver is stood in the middle of the road, lit by Adrian's headlights, urging them to stop. The song cuts out, and not even Rambunctious Rico speaks.

The driver comes to the window. It is the fragile man-child with the suit too big for him. He spreads his arms around the car as if he could hold it back if Adrian tried to drive off.

"Can we help you?"

"What?" The man-child looks at Adrian, then Kurt, then to his own broken down car. "Oh. No. Well, yes actually. Could either of you tell me the time?"

"We were on the same bus this morning." Kurt says, examining the many creases of the man-child's suit.

"No we weren't." He insists, looking cartoonishly suspicious, his eyes darting around, sweat pouring down his face.

"Yeah, it was the 75."

"I don't know any busses."

A moment passes in which no one speaks, and only the gentle wheeze of Adrian's car can be heard.

"It's just gone 8:30." Adrian says.

"What? Oh, right, yes." The man-child starts to walk away but quickly turns on his heels. "8:30 exactly?"

"No, just gone."

"Gone by how much?"

"Two minutes."

"So you're saying its 8:32"

"Well, it's 8:33 now."

"8:33 exactly? How sure are you that it's 8:33. Your eyesight isn't what it used to be."

"What are you on about?"

The man-child takes a step back and thinks for a moment. He takes a small black notebook from his inside pocket and skims through it, turning to one page, then another, then back to the first, then back again. He closes the book, puts it in his pocket, looks at his broken down car, looks at Adrian, looks at Kurt, looks at the car radio.

"Right, well, fine. I'll just move my car."

"Isn't it broken down?"

"I've told you once, and I'll tell you again, Kurt, I don't know anything about busses."

The man-child storms over to his car, looking scorned and frustrated. By the time Adrian and Kurt are able to move on, Rambunctious Rico is playing The Busboys once again.

The ginger kid is back. He sits in a stream of light coming from an open window. The cat is desperate now. He walks in circles, wondering how his life has got to this point, questioning whether he was ever cut out for catching dots. The kid laughs maniacally, waving the pen and calling the animal a 'fucking retard'. The cat looks from kid to dot to kid to dot, not having any sort of grasp on the mind games at play. At his wits end, Kurt opens the window.

"Get a life!" He yells. The kid casually turns and laughs louder, shifting the pens beam so it points directly into Kurt's face. He closes the window and the curtains, but still he can see the dot when he closes his eyes.

Kurt looks at his reflection in the bathroom mirror and wonders if he might cry. Deep down he knows he won't. His dad was right about him needing a shave.

He thinks back to the day he first walked into his local Department of Assisted Suicide building. He put on a pair of old, mud-stained Converse and realised one of the soles had started to peel off. He tried walking around the flat in them but whenever he took a step, the sole would fold into a flap under his foot and he'd stumble forwards. He tried to listen to music but his headphones inexplicably cut out. The following day they were working again, but at the time it felt like a real catastrophe.

He picks up the photos he left out earlier that day and in the process of putting them away he comes across a CD that has fallen down Henry Hoover's back. The name of the artist doesn't ring any bells, but the man on the cover looks familiar. It is signed, 'to Kurt, my biggest fan'.

Just as Kurt inserts the disc into his CD player he hears a knock. He doesn't move for a moment, just looks at his door, trying to mimic the confused facial expressions he imagines a normal person would make upon hearing an unexpected guest at this late hour. Another knock comes, louder this time, then another. They come more frequently and with increasing volume. He goes to look through his peephole, but changes his mind at the memory of his stepmum doing the same. Instead, he simply opens the door.

The man child is soaked, though it has not been raining. It takes Kurt a second to realise its all sweat. He wears Quiet Frank's signature horrified expression and struggles to catch his breath.

"It's just gone ten." Kurt says, unprompted. "If you want me to be more specific I'll have to find my phone."

The man-child puts his hand up, still unable to speak through panicked gasps. In his other hand he holds a bin liner that is full to burst. In spite of the man-child's fragility, he seems to hold it up with relative ease.

"Oh, Kurt. I'm ever so sorry, Kurt. Oh, I've really buggered this one up Kurt."

Kurt considers asking how the man-child knows his name, but he knows that stupid questions get stupid answers, and he's not taking his chances.

"Oh, Kurt, it's a shambles. We're losing more guys every day, Kurt. They're all just so depressed, Kurt."

Kurt becomes acutely aware that the ginger kid is staring at them, pointing his pen at the back of the man-child's head.

"You can come in if you want."

The man child walks around the flat as though it were his own. Kurt is amazed that he instantly knows where to find the biscuits.

"I've really shafted myself this time, Kurt. Really gone and shafted myself. I never thought I was cut out for the job. I told them, Kurt." He sits down, then gets right back up again, goes into another cupboard and gets out a bottle of wine. "Shafted. Shafted. Shafted."

For a while the two of them sit on opposite sides of the living room, the man-child muttering about being shafted, Kurt eyeing up the biscuits but not moving to take them.

"I only started a few weeks ago." The man-child says, having now gained some composure.

"Started what?"

"Working at Dignity. They barely gave me any training, Kurt. Like I said, everyone's getting so depressed. They all stopped coming into work. They needed all the help they could get, Kurt. I was just trying to help. But the job was just too big, Kurt. The job was just too damn big."

The bin bag is within Kurt's reach, and he cranes his neck trying to see what's inside it.

"He's the biggest rock star in the world, Kurt. Well, he was. The casual listeners are easy enough, you know, the old 'what's the time' routine. But what about the families, Kurt? What about the poor mother? Eh? There are tricks that take years to learn, Kurt. I don't know the tricks, Kurt."

Without thinking about it, Kurt moves towards the bin bag. Yet again, he's letting his body do the work, though he's fairly sure this isn't what he would do if even if he was a person who did things. The man-child watches him do this, but doesn't react.

"And the real die-hard fans, such as yourself. Well it's hard not to think of it as immoral, Kurt. There's whole chapters of your life built around this guy, Kurt."

Inside the bag is a variety of merchandise. Hats, t-shirts, posters, all with pictures of a man Kurt has come to recognise. The man-child picks up the CD case from the coffee table where it sits, open and discless.

"Biggest fan, eh? Hate to break it to you, Kurt, but I beg to differ. You should have seen this girl in Northampton I was just dealing with. You think you're obsessed."

"Obsessed with what?"

"Well that's promising, at least. Anyway, she was mad, Kurt. She had nothing but wall to wall posters. All the tat: mugs, badges, even ash trays. Ash trays, Kurt! She'd even made her own stuff. Forks and spoons with little emblems she'd designed. The house was a shrine, Kurt. By the time I was done, the place was bare. Now that's depressing. At least I managed to sort the shitting radio stations there, though."

Kurt unravels a poster that still has remnants of Blu Tack on its back. The man-child walks over to the CD player, where the disc has already been inserted. He takes it out but then, seeing Kurt's confusion, puts it back in.

"I was always more of a Busboys fan, Kurt. In fact, I was listening to them on the radio this morning and I thought to myself how amazing it would be to hear 'Cleaning The Table Of Love' for the first time all over again. Nothing like the first time, eh, Kurt?"

The man-child presses play, Kurt drops the bag, and everything makes sense.

"By the way, Kurt, would you be able to tell me the time?"

DEATH AND THE SALESMAN

Travis has booked four appointments in his first hour. That's unheard of. Gloria, Tina, and Beulah are hunched between Christopher's desk and a fake bamboo tree. Here, they can get the best view of Travis without him spotting them.

"He'll have half the country dead by teatime."

Both Beulah and Gloria make a point of saying how attractive they think Travis is. Others around the office have said the same. Christopher doesn't see it, but he also knows what they say about him, and he gets the feeling that they wouldn't value his opinion on the matter much. Christopher tries not to pay attention to the women whispering by his desk. He has his own work to be getting on with. He even has Beulah's work to be getting on with. He's currently filling in her client forms. They were on his desk this morning with a note telling him that, if only he would pull his weight, he wouldn't have to take on extra responsibilities.

Christopher notices Rex approaching before anyone. Beulah and Gloria catch on quick enough to make a speedy retreat back to their desks. Tina, however, is in a world of her own. She continues watching Travis on the phone, his feet up on his desk. Christopher can see she's agitated by his presence. Rex clears his throat, giving Tina a start. She jumps up, apologises, and moves on.

"Christopher." Rex says, "I wanted to have a quick word."

Rex and Christopher have had several 'quick words' over the course of the last few weeks. Most of the time Christopher just nods along. When his boss finally reaches the point, that Christopher hasn't been performing as well as he should, Christopher responds,

"Well, it's not for lack of trying."

And this is the truth. But, of course, Rex just sees the figures at the end of the day. And as far as Rex is concerned, the figures speak for themselves.

"There was a time," the boss says, "not too long ago, that you were my top man! I was ready to get you back on house calls! On your own this time! What happened?"

Christopher shrugs, the boss sighs, and this is how their quick word ends. The same way it always does.

He finishes Beulah's client forms and gets back on the phone, something he's only partially grateful for. At least doing the paperwork gave him an excuse for not making any appointments. First on the list is a Mrs Mae Everett. He reads over the notes, and recognises the name of the street. Even if he didn't, he'd know it would be an affluent neighbourhood. The door-to-door canvassers who get these names and numbers know who to target. The phone doesn't ring for long before a man picks up. He sounds frustrated, but this doesn't bother Christopher. He's used to it.

"Hello, I was looking to speak to a Mrs Everett."

"What do you want?"

"I'm afraid that information is between myself and Mrs Everett." He tries to say this in a sympathetic manner, but the man doesn't seem to notice or care.

"I'll get her now. But she's watching her show, so don't be surprised if she's in a mood."

Christopher can hear shuffling as the man walks through what must be a very big house. It's a while before he hears the voice of Mrs Everett.

"Yes, yes, yes, what is it? I'm watching my show, you know?"

"Hello, Mrs Everett. This is Christopher calling from Dignity."

"Oh, for crying out loud. I've already told you I'm not interested. I spoke to a woman just the other week and said so."

"I'm sorry, Mrs Everett, I wasn't aware we'd spoken to you so recently."

"I told her I'm on my way out. I don't need any help."

"But you did request a quote?"

"Yes, three months ago. But no one came! I waited in and everything."

"Oh dear, well I am sorry to hear that, Mrs Everett. But we are in the area at the moment, and all our quotes are valid for twelve months. No obligation. And since we didn't manage to get out to you last time I'd be happy to apply a 20% discount on all services."

Christopher can hear Gloria and Tina on their phones, going through the same script. They're always in the area, and always happy to apply a 20% discount.

"I hardly have any family, you know? Just my two sons. And I think they'd have an easy enough time forgetting me when I'm gone, even without the help of your little task force."

"I'm sure that's not true, Mrs Everett."

"Yes, you'd have an easy job with me. Still, it wouldn't help the cost, would it? I've heard about the prices you charge."

"Actually, if it really is just your two sons, it would be, I feel, a very reasonable price. Of course, there are neighbours and acquaintances and people who know your sons to consider. But you'd be amazed at some of the feats we're able to pull off. Just last week we had a man who had seventeen sisters.

Each sister had seventeen daughters. Can you believe that?"

"A big payday for you, I suppose."

"We had forty men on the job."

"And how did it turn out?" Mrs Everett asks, sounding interested for the first time.

"To be perfectly honest, Mrs Everett, it was a bit of a disaster. The client changed his mind at the last minute. Which is fine, of course, but we had got ahead of ourselves. He's still alive, but only seven of his sisters and three of his nieces can remember his name."

Christopher can see Rex stood in the doorway of his office. The boss is staring back at him, eyes narrow, mouth parted.

"Does that kind of thing happen often?"

Rex raises his eyebrows. He can get them farther up his head than eyebrows ought to go.

"Not at all. People don't often change their minds."

"Well, Christopher, as nice as it has been speaking to you, I need to go. The adverts are about to finish."

Before Christopher can say anything further, Mrs Everett hangs up the phone. He sinks into his chair, and Rex raises his arms, as if to say, 'what was all that about?'

Don's phone rests on top of an open tub of butter. He hums along to the music that's been playing for the half hour he has been on hold. He has it memorised now. It's a piece played softly on a classical guitar. For a while it was getting on his nerves, but he's settled into it now. He's making a cup of coffee very slowly by pouring tiny amounts of water from the kettle onto a teaspoon and then dropping it into his mug. It isn't a particular method he is fond of. It just kills time.

Don's mother is upstairs, in Cliff's old bedroom. That room has the big TV. Bigger even than the TV in the lounge. She's using it to watch *Austin*. It's the only show she watches, and she tunes in every week. She's waiting to find out who killed Boris Bold. Now that Boris is dead, her favourite character is Marcy, who owns the trailer park. When the episodes end on a cliffhanger, as they do every week, Don's mother becomes infuriated. She screams and curses and moves to the next room along, Don's own childhood bedroom, so she can vent her frustration by breaking things.

Finally, Don hears a click, and the Doctor is there at the other end of the line. The doctor spends some time clearing his throat, which quickly develops into revolting retching noises, then a hacking cough. When he stops, he speaks clear and calm, as though nothing had happened.

"Mr Everett! Thanks for returning my call."

"Are you alright, Doctor Brooke? That sounds like a nasty cough."

"Yes, yes, yes. I cut my leg shaving yesterday. It should clear up in no time. Now what is it you wanted?"

"You called me. You left me a message."

"Yes! It was about your mother. How is she?"

"I'm not totally sure, to be honest with you. It's hard to tell. She's always been moody. But she has been spending a lot of time in bed. She's there now. Watching *Austin*."

"Did they find out who burned down the courthouse?"

"It was Wesley."

"That rat bastard!"

"That was weeks ago. Now they're trying to find out who killed Boris Bold."

"Boris is dead?"

"Yes."

"My God! But what does that mean for Tiny Tony and all the boys at the orphanage?"

"Can we get back to my mum for a moment?"

"I'm sorry, Mr Everett, but what you have told me today has shaken me to my very core. I'll have to call you back."

"But–"

"Please, Don! Let me grieve!"

Don goes back to the kettle, pouring the water onto the spoon, then into the mug. The water is cold now. He'll have to start again. He hears the sound of drawers being pulled from their units and then thrown to the ground. By the time he gets up to his old room, his mother is tearing the curtains from the rail.

Christopher is sat at his desk with nothing to do. He's supposed to be handling the inbound calls, but nothing is getting through to him. It's all diverted to Tina and Travis. They keep exchanging flirtations glances. She rolls her eyes as if to say, 'is this guy gonna let us kill him or what?' And he rolls his own in response as if to say, 'tell me about it'.

Gloria and Beulah are across the room, procrastinating. They phone people they know will never answer. Clients who seemed eager when they asked for their quotes, but who are now ignoring the repeated calls or, more likely, have done the job themselves. They let the phones ring out as long as possible while they carry out the same conversations they always have.

"Dragging today, isn't it?"

"Just one of those days."

Every day is 'one of those days', as far as Gloria and Beulah are concerned. Everything they say falls from their lips with a huff and a sigh.

"Got anything nice lined up for tea?"

"Daniel is going to make spag bol. And you?"

"Fish supper, I reckon."

"Ooh, not for me, thank you very much."

Christopher answers his phone. He doesn't know how long it's been ringing. He was staring into space. Before he can start reading his script, the woman starts talking. She's not in hysterics, like a lot of the callers they get. She doesn't even sound particularly upset. She gets straight to the point, with the stern tone of a teacher faced with an unruly class.

"This is Mae Everett. I spoke to one of your people a while ago about getting a quote and I'd like for you to send someone out to provide me with one. I've had enough, you see."

"Of course, Mrs Everett. I do remember our conversation. When would be convenient for you?"

"I'm here all day. Every day."

"I can try and get someone out in a few hours. Around four?"

"That's fine. My son will let you in."

And just like that, she's gone. Christopher fills out Mrs Everett's form and takes it straight to Rex.

"I can't believe it!" He says, "This is good, Christopher. Really great. We've been calling this woman for months. When does she want us out?"

"Four."

"Today? Oh, sugar. Harry is off today. Don't fret. I'll sort something out. I'll let you know what happens."

Christopher takes the long way back to his desk. He gets a can of cola from the vending machine. It's a brand he's never heard of. It tastes revolting, so he throws it out. He goes to the water cooler, fills up one of the paper cones and drinks. He keeps the cone and fills it twice more while he waits to see if anyone will walk by. He wishes he could go home. End the day on a high note.

The doors to the lift open and Barney Saggs walks out. Barney started working at Dignity at the same time as Christopher. They went through training together, but Barney ended up doing debriefings. Christopher smiles at Barney. Barney doesn't smile back. He walks straight past.

Christopher hears a rustling and turns just in time to see Travis fishing the cola out of the bin. He drinks it in two gulps and smiles.

"Free." He says.

He stands by Christopher at the cooler, filling up one cone, drinking it, throwing away the cone, and filling another.

"How are you finding the job?" Christopher asks.

"Oh, it's great. That Tina is a nice piece of ass, right?"

Christopher finds it hard to suppress his surprise that someone could really talk like that. Receiving no response or further questioning, Travis starts to walk away. He stops in his tracks, though, when he sees Rex heading over.

"Big boss man!" He says, and gives Rex a special hi-five they must have worked on together. Christopher is grateful not to be in on it. The boss smiles wide, grateful for the public display of friendship.

"I'm glad I've caught you both. Now, it's not totally ideal, but Harry is off and I can't get through to Marvin. He's been on a house call for two hours now. Anyway, I was hoping you two could go out to see Mrs Everett. Travis, you've been absolutely excellent so far. And Christopher, you've done this before. I reckon if you put your heads together you can work it out."

Christopher wants to protest but Travis agrees before he has the chance.

"Great. Christopher, you know this one is a big deal, but Travis really has something going. If you can run him through the basics, I'm sure he'll be able to deliver the pitch."

The house is big, but not absurdly so. Especially when compared to the ones around it. Ike Wardell, the celebrity chef, lives next door. His house is three times the size of Mrs Everett's, and looks like a giant burger. Mrs Everett's house, on the other hand, is house shaped.

A man answers the door, and Christopher recognises his voice from the phone call. The man, in turn, seems to recognise Christopher and Travis. Or, at least, recognises their dark blue uniforms.

"What do you want?"

"We have an appointment with Mrs Everett." Travis says, grinning.

"Oh? This is the first I'm hearing about it."

"We're a little early. We had arranged to arrive at four."

Don looks at his watch. It is two minutes to four.

"Right, well I suppose you can come in."

As the men enter the house, an elderly, red-haired woman comes up the path behind them.

"Don! I thought you'd left already."

"Hi, Karen, my train isn't until tomorrow."

Karen, who had been the one to inform Don of his mother's sudden depression, eyes Christopher and Travis with great suspicion. She too appears to recognise the uniform.

"Right. Well it was nice to see you after so long. Perhaps your brother will call round some time."

"I wouldn't have thought so," Don says, trying his best to sound respectful, "Cliff passed away a few years ago."

"No he didn't."

"Yes he did."

"Oh, no he didn't."

"Oh, yes he did."

"Christopher, I saw him three weeks ago."

"Where?"

"Just over in Tarraby. You know, that boy is so cool. There's no other word for it."

Travis clears his throat, and all heads turn towards him.

"Is it alright if we go inside?"

"Right. Yes. OK. I'll tell mum you called, Karen."

"It was just to remind her about *Austin* being pushed forward."

"Right. Yes. I'll remind her."

In Mrs Everett's house, all the walls are painted different colours. Sometimes it's only a slightly different shade of the same colour, which Christopher finds unsettling. Nothing here seems purely functional. A lamp in the corner of the room is not just a lamp but a lamp in the shape of an elephant, whose trunk acts as a switch. The sofa is not a regular sofa, but a snake sofa, which bends and twists in peculiar places. The coffee table is not a coffee table at all, but a great wooden tiger, whose back is arched so that you'd hardly be able to balance anything on it. The whole place makes Christopher feel nauseous. Travis seems to like it though, or at least that's what he says to Don.

"Well isn't this just magnificent."

Don doesn't respond. He looks to be in shock. When they go upstairs he absentmindedly leads them to the wrong room twice before they get to Mrs Everett. She's laid there with the quilt pulled right up to her neck. She turns to the men with a look that expresses nothing whatsoever.

"These men say they have an appointment with you."

"Yes."

No one says a thing for a moment. Christopher looks at Travis, who looks at Don, who looks at Mrs Everett. Mrs Everett looks straight up at the ceiling.

"Mum?"

"Yes?"

"I just spoke to Karen. She says she saw Cliff."

"Yes."

"Did you know?"

"Yes."

"But Cliff is dead."

"No."

"No?"

"No."

Don rests against the door jamb, lets out a sigh, and rubs his forehead. He turns to walk out the room, but ends up doing a full circle.

"She also said to remind you that *Austin* got pushed forward."

"Yes. No! What?"

"So they can show the game."

"Oh, shitting hell."

Mrs Everett throws her quilt across the room as she jumps up. She darts out the room with the speed of someone much younger than herself. The men aren't sure what to do. They hear the theme from *Austin* coming from the big TV. Don leaves the two men in the hall and retreats back downstairs. If Christopher had his way, they would follow, but Travis pushes forward, into Cliff's bedroom.

"So, Mrs Everett," Travis says, "would you like me to go through the different packages we provide?"

Mrs Everett says nothing.

"Mrs Everett? If it's something you'd like to go forward with we can set the wheels in motion as soon as you'd like. Even within the next few hours."

Mrs Everett says nothing.

"Mrs Everett? How about our Premium Package? We can plan your funeral, and use the wake to debrief everyone in attendance. Two birds, one stone. Mrs Everett? What's with this woman?"

Mrs Everett shushes Travis, but he doesn't seem to notice. He takes out a file and reads all the information he has on the different packages. Ways they might bring her life to an end, and ways they might deal with the aftermath. Mrs Everett tries again to silence him, and then for a third time. She shushes with increasing intensity. Christopher worries she might snap, but once she realises he won't shut up, she appears to accept it. She doesn't look at either of the men, and turns the volume up. Still, Travis carries on talking. Christopher can't help but respect his determination. But even he stops listening to Travis after a while. He turns instead to the enormous TV. He's never watched *Austin* before, but as Travis rambles on, Christopher finds himself more and more invested. He can see the appeal. He's already rooting for a teenage boy who wants to become a dancer, in spite of the wishes of his stern, conservative father. When Christopher does eventually turn his attention back to Travis, he sees his co-worker has turned red. He's wiping sweat off his forehead and shaking with the fury of a man who has reached his wit's end.

"Maybe we should go." Christopher says.

Travis takes a few slow, deep breaths, but doesn't lose any of his redness.

"I need to use the bathroom."

"Out and to the right." says Mrs Everett. Travis leaves the room, and Christopher thinks he can hear him making pathetic whimpers of defeat in the hallway.

Mrs Everett and Christopher can finally sit in silence, waiting with anticipation to see if the dancing boy's father will discover the tutu he has hidden in his bedroom drawer. Or if the dancing boy will discover the tutu his father keeps in his own drawer. But just as both drawers are simultaneously pulled open, it cuts to an ad break, and they're suddenly hearing about a new type of window cleaner that gets windows so clean, you won't know there's a window there at all.

"My friend Karen tried that."

"Does it work?"

"Too well. Her nephew keeps walking into the patio door."

Christopher laughs, but looks over at Mrs Everett to see she has a straight face. He wonders if he's offended her, but she's not looking at him. She keeps her eyes on the TV, her legs twitching, body hunched forward, waiting for the show to come back on. Her expression isn't the same as it had been moments before. When the handsome Detective Hale was working the case, searching for Boris Bold's killer, Mrs Everett was wide-eyed and open-mouthed. Now she looks as though she's struggling to keep her head raised and has a thousand-yard stare. Christopher has seen people like this many times before. Clients who take the first package they are offered and ask that the process begin immediately.

"I'd never seen this show before."

"It's awful."

"Why do you watch it?"

"I want to know what happens."

"You have any idea what went on with Boris Bold?"

Mrs Everett finally turns to Christopher. She looks him up and down before answering.

"My friend Karen thinks is was Gunter. You know, the caretaker at the school? Some people are saying it's going to be his daughter. That she killed him for what he did to David." She leans over a little on her bed, edging closer to where Christopher sits. "But if you ask me, I reckon it was the detective."

Christopher can't help but let out a little gasp, feeling strangely startled by the mere suggestion.

"But he seems so nice. So determined to find the killer."

"He never said anything to anyone about knowing Lydia Bold. Why would he keep that a secret?"

"I think it was the woman with the short hair."

"Marcy? From the trailer park?"

"That's the one."

"Don't make me laugh."

But Mrs Everett is already laughing. She laughs so much that Don can hear her from downstairs. It startles him, this strange noise he doesn't remember ever hearing before. It's enough to distract him from his conversation. The man on the other end of the phone starts wearily calling out to him,

"Hello? Hello? Are you still there?"

"Yes. Sorry. So can it be arranged?"

"I can ask him, but what should I say it is you want?"

"I don't know. Can't you make something up? You'd be doing me a big favour?"

"Favour?"

Don sighs. "I'll buy you dinner when I get back. Anywhere you like."

"Pedro's?"

"Sure."

"I don't like it there. The music is too loud."

"Then why did you suggest it?"

"What about that new Chinese place?"

"Can't we discuss it when I get back?"

As he puts the phone down, Christopher and Travis make their way down the winding flight of stairs. Travis doesn't seem any less perturbed by the visit. He doesn't have to explain himself to Don.

"Difficult, isn't she?"

"She's a real character." Christopher says, which makes Travis cringe.

"Was she laughing just then?"

"Oh, I think she had a good laugh," says Travis, "a right good laugh at our expense."

He walks out ahead of Christopher, unable to keep up the act any longer. Half an hour with Mrs Everett has changed him, and Christopher doesn't know if he'll recover any time soon.

Fred calls this part of the city a 'creative hub'. To Don it just looks like a shithole. The buildings seem like they would collapse in a strong wind. There are warehouses that look abandoned with signs indicating they are in fact used as offices. Don doesn't know how anyone could work in that kind of environment. It's a far stretch from his own office, with clear white walls and a desk that cost more than the big TV at his mum's house.

Don carries a piece of paper, on which he has written an address and directions given to him by Fred over the phone. They have led him to this corner, but he sees no building resembling the one his friend described. He wonders if Fred would intentionally send him on a wild goose chase.

Don is ready to give up when he sees a spotty teenager with a backpack walk out of a big metal door. The door hadn't seemed like a door at all before it was opened. He shows the boy the information on the paper, and the boy tells him he has the right place. The big metal door leads to two more doors. Then, to Don's chagrin, he has to crawl under a heavy purple curtain, finding no seam to part. Finally, he ascends three flights of stairs and arrives at the office of Paul Owens. The office, if you could call it that, is an enormous room. It's cold and dark and damp. Paul sits at his desk at the far end. By the entrance is a woman at her own desk which, on closer inspection, is an upturned cardboard box with reams of tissue paper laid on it as a makeshift cloth.

"What do you want?" She asks.

"Is that Paul Owens?"

"Who wants to know?"

"I have an appointment with him."

"Well I'm his assistant and I've never heard of you."

"I didn't say my name."

"What's your name?"

"Donald."

"I've never heard of you."

Don can see the woman has a list titled, 'Tuesday Schedule'. There is only one item listed, 'meeting with Donald Everett'. The assistant folds it up and puts it in her pocket.

"One second," she says, "I have to answer this."

She picks up the phone, though it didn't ring. In fact, Don sees that it is clearly a toy phone for children, with googly eyes and a big smile.

"Hello. Yes. Yes. Yes. No. Yes. Oh, God, no. Yes. About three inches. Yes. Perfect. I'll tell him now." She looks up at Don. "Paul says he's busy."

Don ignores her and walks over to the man at the far end. The assistant doesn't do or say anything to try and stop him.

As Don approaches Paul Owens, two things become clear. First, that Paul Owens has the same desk Don has. Which seems ludicrous to him. Second, that Paul Owens isn't a man, but a boy. A boy, if Don was to guess, of about twelve or thirteen. Still, he's dressed like a working man, has bags under his eyes and the weary look of someone who has toiled three nights with no sleep.

"Are you Paul Owens?"

"Yes."

"The Paul Owens who writes for *Austin*?"

"That's me."

"You know Fred?"

"Of course! How is he?"

"He said he knew you from school?"

"Yes."

Don doesn't say anything, but looks at the boy in a way that conveys his disbelief and suspicion.

"I went to school with his son. Before I got the job, of course."

"Right."

"Fred tells me you were looking to get some writing tips."

"He did?"

"That's not the case?"

"No."

"Oh."

Paul Owens sips his coffee, and types something on his computer. "So what did you want?"

"I want you to hold off revealing who killed Boris Bold."

Paul Owens looks at Don with the same suspicion Don had greeted him with. Don doesn't like how it feels on the other end. He almost feels bad for not trusting the boy. But he remembers the ordeal with the assistant. He looks back to see that she has gone. As has the tissue and toy phone. Only the cardboard box remains.

"I read in *TV Now* that you plan to reveal the killer soon. I'm willing to pay for you to push it back."

"For how long?"

"If I had my way, it would be indefinitely. But we can come to an arrangement. At least a month."

"A month?"

"I can give you three thousand."

"I'll take your money, but I don't know how I'm supposed to convince the studio."

"Don't look at me, I'm not the writer."

Paul Owens turns in his chair and looks up to the dirty windows high on the back wall.

"Do I get the money now?"

Don takes an envelope out of his coat and removes a handful of cash before handing the rest to Paul Owens, knowing the boy will see how far he was willing to go.

"Out of interest, who did kill Boris Bold?"

"Marcy. From the trailer park. I thought it was obvious."

There are strict rules at Dignity against hanging up on potential customers. But Christopher is starting to feel like trying his luck. Whoever is on the other end is giving him the silent treatment.

"Hello?"

Still nothing. Tina, Beulah and Gloria are chatting away, having their own individual conversations without bothering to respond to each other.

"I had an omelet. At eight of an evening! Can you believe that?"

"Just one of those days."

"And she asked if I would buy her child! Who do I look like? Rumpelforeskin?"

Travis is at the other end of the room, sounding jittery and uncomfortable on the phone.

"Yes. But. No, it's OK. Of course. And we, uh. Oh, is that right? I'm sorry."

He's lost all his confidence, and his time at Dignity may soon be over.

"Hello?" Christopher says again. "Is anyone there?"

"Is that Christopher?" The woman says, tentatively.

"It is."

"Oh, thank God. I was worried I'd got through to one of the others again."

"Mrs Everett? Changed your mind again, have you?"

"No, no, no. I wanted to know if you'd caught up with *Austin*?"

"I have, actually. I watched the whole thing last week."

"Very good! So do you want to call round this Wednesday?"

"I don't know how much Don would like me coming back."

"Oh, I'm sick of the sight of that boy. Ever since he found out I'm leaving all my money to his brother he's been falling over himself trying to get me to change the will."

"I'd love to, Mae, but I'll be working."

"Have it your way." She says, and abruptly hangs up the phone.

Christopher spends the rest of the day staring at the clock, waiting for calls that never come. Just as he's packing his things to leave, Rex walks over, asking for another 'quick word'. And finally, Christopher feels his time is up.

"I just had Mrs Everett on the phone. She wants to make arrangements."

"Oh?"

"She knows what she wants, and she's ready to iron out the details. She asked for you specifically. You must have left an impression. You'll be heading down there at five on Wednesday."

Driving alone to Mrs Everett's house, Christopher takes the wrong exit off a roundabout and finds himself stuck behind four ambulances that block the road ahead. A double decker bus has hit the railway bridge and the roof has been torn off. There are medics running around, bodies on stretchers, and people sat on the side of the road in tears. One man has blood pouring from his mouth. His teeth are scattered all around. He gathers them up and rattles them at a medic who tries to calmly explain that there isn't much he can do about it right now.

As Christopher steps out of his car, he hears a roar and a screech. A motorcycle comes speeding down the road. The rider, not spotting the blockage in time, hits the back of Christopher's car and goes flying over the handlebars. He rolls over the roof and lands in a heap near the toothless man. The man doesn't seem to notice, and the medics don't seem to care. They've all got their hands full.

Christopher rushes over to help the rider, but he's already back on his feet.

"Woah, dude! That was sick. Did you see that?"

"Are you OK?"

"You tell me." He lifts his visor and puts a hand over his face. "How's this looking?"

The rider is approaching middle age, with long blonde hair and eyes that are an unnaturally bright shade of green.

"Looks alright to me."

"Then we're all good. You're gonna have to have that looked at, though." He puts his hand to Christopher's face. Christopher looks at his reflection in his wing mirror and sees he has blood pouring from a gash that runs from the top of his forehead to just above his left eye. He has no idea how it happened, and feels no pain.

"Shitting hell."

"Yeah, that's pretty gnarly. Did I do that?"

"I don't think so."

"I hope not. I want us to be cool, you know. I want this experience to bring us together. Not drive us apart."

Christopher looks confused, but the rider doesn't explain any further. He just smiles and picks up his bike.

"Here's my details. In case there's any damage."

The rider hands Christopher a black card with silver writing. It says his name is Cliff Richard Everett, and that he is a 'professional sidewalk surfer, chick inspector, and life coach'.

"You want me to take you to the hospital?"

Christopher declines and gets back in his car. The toothless man is trying to put his teeth back in. He isn't doing a good job.

Christopher takes the day off work, though he feels fine. His face is stitched up and as he walks around town he gets some strange looks. One child runs crying into her mother's arms.

He stops by a pawn shop. Clips from *Austin* are playing on the TV in the window. It's only now that he remembers he had been on his way to see Mrs Everett. He got caught up in the madness of the accident and hospital visit. The next clip shows Marcy from the trailer park shooting Boris Bold. Christopher looks away, annoyed that he has spoiled it for himself.

As he turns, he catches a glimpse of Barney Saggs. He is hiding down the side of a vegan cafe. Only his head is visible and he's looking in Christopher's direction. When they lock eyes, Barney quickly moves out of sight. After a moment he walks back out into the street, whistling, with his hands in his pockets, looking up to the sky. Then, seeing Christopher, he suddenly jumps back and opens his mouth wide with feigned surprise.

"Christopher! Fancy seeing you here! How are you, mate? How have you been?"

Christopher is taken aback by the display, and doesn't know how to respond. He hears the doors of the pawn shop open behind him, and feels a hand on his shoulder. Barney takes a passport photo from his pocket.

"I was hoping I'd see you, actually. I was wondering if you could help me. Do you recognise this woman?"

As Christopher looks at the photo he feels something digging into his back. Then a sharp pinch. Mae Everett looks so very upset. Marcy was her new favourite.

Barney does something strange with his hands. He says something. And for the life of him, Christopher can't make out what it is.

CRYING WOLF

There's a felt-tip mural on one side of the bus shelter. Little Rodney examines it as though it were an exhibition piece. It's the head of a dog on a cat's body. To its left, the cat's severed head, and to the right, the dogs decapitated body. Little Rodney imagines a history for this piece. It develops in his mind so quickly and in such vivid detail that he ends up almost believing it himself.

Little Rodney is so lost in thought that he doesn't hear the old woman approaching. When she is finally behind him, breathing down his neck, he jumps in shock. The woman doesn't even look at Little Rodney, though. She's staring at the mural. She looks exhausted, and it seems as though the image of the cat-dog is only making things worse. The woman is short and slender. She wears a grey anorak and carries two Lidl bags full of shopping in each hand. She sighs, puts down the bags, takes a pair of glasses out her jacket pocket, and squints, careful to absorb every detail of the grotesque artwork. She makes a sound that Little Rodney can't make sense of. Confusion, disgust and indignation all in a single grunt. She stares at it a moment longer before eventually turning to Little Rodney for answers.

"Commissioned by the council." He says.

She makes the sound again, louder this time. Little Rodney still can't interpret the meaning of it.

"I'll be writing to the paper about this."

The woman puts her glasses back in her pocket, lifts her shopping, and walks away.

The bus arrives, and the driver confirms that it's heading where Little Rodney needs to go.

Big Rodney isn't expecting his son at the farm. But Little Rodney knows it will be alright.

Big Rodney stands outside the big house, watching Little Rodney trudge through the muddy field. He occasionally raises his coffee to his lips, but doesn't sip. It's getting dark, and he's only just awake.

"Fancy seeing you here," Big Rodney calls out, having determined that his son is close enough that he won't have to raise his voice too much. Something he never likes to do.

"Thought I'd pay a visit. Just for a bit. I hope that's OK?"

Big Rodney can tell something isn't right, but he doesn't ask. He puts an arm around his son and leads him inside.

"You'll have to entertain yourself, I'm afraid. It's a big one tonight."

"Yeah, I heard Rico mention it this morning."

Big Rodney rolls his eyes.

"Did he now? Well I'm doing a whole episode on it. Gonna really get into the details."

"Is there anything I can do to help?"

"Diggman needs some washing done, if you fancied calling round there?"

This isn't the answer Little Rodney hoped for.

Doug Diggman owns the farm. He lives in the small house, which sits just a stone's throw away from the big house. Big Rodney takes care of the old man and his farm. Diggman rarely leaves the comfort of his bed, and absolutely refuses to step foot in the big house. He says it reminds him too much of his mother, who built the big house with the same hands she would use to throttle the young Diggman and his eleven brothers.

The old man is sleeping when Little Rodney enters. The radio on his bedside table is on, and turned up to the highest volume. Little Rodney knows he doesn't have to worry about waking Diggman up. Diggman only ever wakes up when he's good and ready, no matter how hard you may try to stir him.

Little Rodney does a lap of the house, gathering the clothes that are strewn here and there. He puts them in the washing machine, which is as old as he is and almost loud enough to drown out the sound of the radio. Diggman looks just as peaceful as ever.

Just as Little Rodney sits himself on the old leather armchair across from Diggman's bed, he hears the introductory jingle of his father's show.

"Good evening, night owls. This is Restrained Rodney's Bedtime Broadcast. If you managed to catch the end of Rico's show, you might have heard him mention what makes tonight so important. That's right, in just a few hours it will be the seventeenth, which will mark ten years since the start of the Blackout. We will be commemorating this throughout the weekend by revisiting some highlights from mine and Rico's era-defining, 'Dispatches From The Darkness'. We will also field calls about your memories of those troublesome few months back in 2022."

Big Rodney plays a snippet from an old interview with a woman who claims to make candles out of deer fat. As she starts speaking, Diggman wakes up.

"Is that you Rodney?"

"It's Little Rodney."

"Well, I never!" He says, "I haven't seen you in a year, three months, and twelve days."

Diggman has a remarkable memory, which only seems to improve with age, and he takes any opportunity to show it off.

"Is this a repeat of Miss Linda Walgrove's interview from July 23rd 2022?"

"I believe so."

"A right old bore, she was. Plus, it turned out the candles were a front. She just really loved killing deer. Couldn't get enough of it."

"Would you like me to turn it off?"

Diggman nods. With great effort, he shuffles around in an attempt to sit up. But in the end he remains flat on his back with his head angled awkwardly against the pillow.

"You see what your old man did?"

Diggman gestures to a selection of framed pictures on the wall opposite his bed. For as long as Little Rodney can remember, Diggman's walls have been strikingly bare.

"I noticed when I came in. Did you ask him to find them out for you?"

"No. He got them from the big house. They're not so bad, though."

Little Rodney goes in for a closer look. If it wasn't for the clothes, Little Rodney wouldn't be able to tell the photos were taken so long ago. The young Diggman appears as wrinkled and bald at twenty as he is today.

"Is this your wife, then?" Little Rodney asks, pointing to a picture of the old man on his wedding day.

"That was our Betty. We were married for fourteen days before she died. I was never with another."

Little Rodney knows this. He's heard it many times before.

"But, of course, you know that. I've told you many times before. Eight times. Nine now."

Little Rodney is still awake, sat in the kitchen with two hot chocolates, as his father wraps up the show and leaves his basement studio in the early hours of the morning.

When Laura was alive, she would make Big Rodney a coffee every night and a hot chocolate every day. Laura and Big Rodney always put the success of their marriage down to the fact that they hardly saw each other, save for those few hours each day when their paths would cross. She worked early mornings at the Town Hall, he worked late nights on his show.

Laura died one year before Little Rodney left for university. She fell out of a hot-air balloon. The circumstances were relatively unremarkable for the time, as it coincided with a brief hot-air balloon craze. Balloon related deaths were on the rise, and Laura became just another statistic.

It taught Little Rodney a valuable lesson in the dangers of following trends.

"You know," Big Rodney says, "Aaron's little brother used to help out around the farm, but he's run off to Uzbekistan with that puppeteer. So there are jobs that'll need doing if you're sticking around for a while. And, of course, if you're up for it."

Little Rodney nods. He's tired, but knows he couldn't sleep if he tried.

Little Rodney looks up and down the street from his spot outside The Neptune as he waits for Isaac. He considers Isaac the closest thing he has to a friend these days, though they've had no communication since Little Rodney left for university. Still, Little Rodney keeps abreast of what Isaac is up to online. From what he's seen, he feels confident that Isaac is much the same as he ever was. It's a reassuring thought. There are people in Chesterfield that Little Rodney was closer to, but he knows they've already made something of themselves, and he could do without hearing about it.

After forty minutes of waiting, Little Rodney sees Isaac walking up the street towards him. They lock eyes, but Isaac is still far away, down past the bakery at the bottom of the steep incline that leads to the pub. For a while they stare at each other as Isaac slowly approaches. He smiles and doesn't appear uncomfortable at all. This disturbs Little

Rodney, and he wonders whether he's made a huge mistake.

Little Rodney decides to avert his eyes, and settles on watching a middle-aged woman at a nearby cash machine. There's two exceptionally tall, suited men stood behind her, whispering to each other. A third suited man comes out the bank and joins them. They continue their hushed conversation, while keeping an eye on the woman. It seems very suspicious. Little Rodney worries that he might have to defend this woman, a stranger to him.

Then, one of the men puts a hand on the woman's left shoulder, another puts a hand on the woman's right shoulder, and the third circles in front, crouching down to position his face very close to hers. They say something that Little Rodney can't make out, and the woman begins to gently sob. She nods as though she has accepted some inevitable tragedy. She doesn't seem panicked or even particularly uncomfortable under the third man's stare. She reaches into her purse, takes out a passport photo, and gives it to the man on her left. They each make the same peculiar gesture with their hands before walking away.

The middle-aged woman takes her money and dries her eyes. She starts walking down the hill, but abruptly stops, as though she'd forgotten something. Then she turns around and walks the other way.

Little Rodney doesn't have much time to consider the strange interaction before Isaac is beside him, punching his arm a bit too hard.

"Hey man. How's it going? What's good? What's up? What's happening? How's things?"

Isaac tries and fails to execute a secret handshake, long forgotten by Little Rodney. He looks disappointed, but only for a moment.

They get their drinks and sit down. Isaac drags his stool closer to Little Rodney's than he would like.

"So yeah, I've just been doing this and that. Odds and ends. Bits and bobs. Keeping busy. Working hard. Hardly working."

"Oh yeah?"

"Yeah, yeah, yeah. Yes. I'm signed up with this agency. They just drop me a text. An SMS. An SMS on the cell. On the cellular. Sometimes it's just a day. A one time deal. An in-and-out situation. Sometimes it's a couple of weeks. Every now and then a month or two. Once in a blue moon. They're the good ones. That's the ideal. The ideal sitch."

"Oh yeah?"

"Something to do, ain't it? It's a living. It is what it is. Puts food on the table."

"Oh, yeah."

Isaac has the enviable ability to perform well at any given task. He picks up skills with remarkable ease. He'd go far, if he didn't get bored just as easily. He works with speed and efficiency, but if a project takes too long he'll quickly lose passion for it.

There are two men sat in the corner by a pool table. One is thin, the other is fat. The thin man has his hand on the fat man's arm, and rubs it reassuringly. The fat man is enraged. He's shakes his head and puffs his cheeks and sweats and fidgets.

"Why don't we just leave?" The thin man suggests.

"I've got to say something. I can't take it anymore."

The fat man stands up with such force that he knocks his seat over, and storms over to the bar.

"Will you *please* turn that off! I can't stand to listen to him one moment longer!"

It's only as the fat man says this that Little Rodney notices Rambunctious Rico's show playing on the radio. The man behind the bar appears unfazed by the outburst.

"Aw, we always listen to Rico, Gravy. You know that."

"That's the point! I'm sick of it! Everywhere you go, he's there! Why can't we just listen to some music?"

"Rico plays music," says a long-nosed woman at the other end of the bar.

"You keep your long nose out of it, Cam."

"Come on, Gravy," the thin man says, ushering the fat man back to his seat, "let's just simmer down now."

"That's right, listen to small ears and sit down."

The thin man stops in his tracks and looks at Cam, stunned. She doesn't meet his glance, realising that she's taken it too far.

"Small ears? You think I've got small ears?"

"Aw, Cam, why'd you have to say that?" The bartender sighs.

"Gravy, do I have small ears?"

"No, Twiggy. You've got big ears! Tremendous ears!

"You're lying! You don't think I've got big ears at all!"

"I've always said you've got big ears. Everyone says so."

"Has my whole life been a lie?"

Little Rodney suddenly realises that Isaac has been speaking this whole time. Luckily, Isaac doesn't seem to notice that Little Rodney hasn't paid attention. Rambunctious Rico never gets turned off. He talks about the Sadness. The rate of deaths seems to be either increasing or decreasing depending on who you ask and at what time of day. Just before Little Rodney left university, along with all the other students, he saw a girl in his accommodation who had it. Her roommates were getting people from all the other flats to come and have a look. She lay on her bed, clutching her quilt which was pulled right up to her neck. Her eyes were closed and her mouth was wide open. The only indication that she wasn't dead was that she occasionally shook her head and said something that sounded like, 'no', or possibly, 'how'. It was hard to tell with her accent.

"So what made you want to come back?"

Little Rodney finally tunes in to what his friend is saying, and just in time.

"They sent everyone home. They had an outbreak."

"Wow. Wowzers. Wowzers trousers. Wowwowweewaa."

The fat man holds the thin man, and they both shed a tear.

Little Rodney can tell there is something wrong, even before he steps foot in the house. The front door is wide open. He hears the sounds of heavy footsteps and objects being thrown around. When he gets into the hallway, he sees his dad, only briefly, at the top of the stairs, running from one room to another. Little Rodney waits to see if he can deduct what might be happening before anyone has to explain it to him.

Big Rodney appears again, darting out his bedroom and turning sharply to get downstairs. He holds a small suitcase close to his side, and with each step it bangs against his leg.

"Ow. Ow. Ow. Ow. Ow. Hey."

He is temporarily stopped in his tracks by Little Rodney, though he quickly moves the boy to one side and carries on through to the kitchen. He talks to his son with an uncharacteristically raised voice, alternating how loud he has to be depending on where he is in the house in relation to Little Rodney.

"I've got to go. Just for a day or two. Bit of an emergency. It's Rita. You know Auntie Rita? From London? Well she's sick. Sounds a bit grim from what Uncle Ivan has told me."

Little Rodney still doesn't move. He knows he really should do something to help, but is unsure as to how he could.

"Rocky is going to take over while I'm gone. Restrained Rocky. That could work."

"You know, I could always take over. Put my studies to good use."

Big Rodney suddenly stops, holding the handle to the kitchen's French doors, head turned away from Little Rodney.

"No, no, no, no, no. It's fine. No, no, no. It's all good. It's fine. No. Rocky knows his stuff. He knows the buttons."

"I know the buttons."

"Sure, sure, sure. Of course, of course. But no, no, no. It's fine. It's all fine."

"I've got nothing else to do."

"It's a lot of work. It's fine."

"But-"

"No! It's fine! Rocky knows what he's doing. He knows the buttons. It's all sorted."

There's a moment's silence in which both Little and Big Rodney seem as surprised as each other. Then Big Rodney opens the French doors and runs out to the shed.

Little Rodney is woken in the night by the sound of Doug Diggman singing, as he is wont to do of an evening. He goes down to the basement studio. Rocky is in there, turning knobs, clicking buttons, and making adjustments that, though he would never admit it, Little Rodney simply doesn't understand.

Rocky is sixteen. He lives on the neighbouring farm, and takes his bike to the big house every evening to act as a producer on Big Rodney's radio show. He wears a Hawaiian shirt and shorts, even when it rains. He is small for his age and completely hairless. He looks, and occasionally acts like an alien doing a semi-believable impression of a human.

"I'm making a coffee if you want one?" Little Rodney says. Rocky shakes his head.

"Could you get us the pack of FirstQuench out the fridge, though?"

Rocky loves FirstQuench. Little Rodney has never seen anyone drink so much of it and still act so subdued. Some of his fellow students would drink it when they had to pull all-nighters. He once saw a boy write an essay on his laptop while running on a treadmill. A look in his eyes like he was about to go on a murderous rampage.

When Little Rodney returns with the drinks, Rocky is repeating stories his mother would tell him about the Blackout to the audience. His own brother was supposedly conceived in a candlelit room to the sound of Rambunctious Rico. Rocky has the voice of a middle-aged smoker. Still, it's surprisingly soothing. Little Rodney is frustrated by how well he seems to be handing himself on the mic. He rarely even has to look at the bullet pointed topics Big Rodney left for him. He improvises links with a smile, then, when he plays another clip or song, the smile vanishes, and he's back to checking his phone and sipping FirstQuench.

Just as Little Rodney leaves the studio, the phone rings. It's his father.

"How's the show going?"

"It's fine," Little Rodney says, "Rocky seems a bit nervous, but he's powering through."

"Good, good, good, good. Rita hasn't even got a bloody radio. I've never been so cut off. Listen, can you do me a favour and check to see if I locked the shed?

"Can do."

"Thanks. *Infection* is still in there somewhere and I don't want Rocky finding it. That would be a disaster."

"Of course. I thought you'd got rid of it?"

"I meant to but I never could. I knew he couldn't go on the way he was, but you can't deny it was a very fun game. Too fun!"

Little Rodney grabs a torch so he can see his way about in the pitch darkness of the fields. He has some trouble finding the shed, which is far from the big house. He checks the door. It won't open, but the key is still there, hanging from the padlock. He takes the key out and turns to walk back to the big house, but he hesitates. He can still hear Diggman singing, much farther away now. He returns to the shed and removes the padlock. Between some garden tools and a bag filled with old clothes is a cardboard box, sealed with duct tape. Written on the side are the words, 'do not open'.

Rocky leaves the studio just after seven, his hands filled with empty cans. He lines them up in a row on the kitchen counter. Little Rodney sits at the dining table watching this, frustrated that the boy won't make the short journey to the recycling bin.

"I'm off home," Rocky says. "I'll see you tomorrow."

"On your way out could you check to see if the shed door is closed? I thought I heard it banging a minute ago."

Rocky looks at Little Rodney for a moment, confused.

"Yeah, sure."

Little Rodney stands outside with his coffee, as evening sets in once again. He's waits to see if Rocky will show, unsure whether he wants him to or not. He wonders if he's made a big mistake.

A figure approaches, walking slow up the long path to the big house. Little Rodney can't tell who it is, though he's sure it's not Rocky. He worries that it might be his father, returning unannounced and early. He looks over to Diggman's shack and is startled to see that the old man is outside. He's crouched over a plot of flowers at the front of the small house.

"Doug? Are you alright?"

"Wonderful." He replies, not turning around.

"What are you doing up and about?"

"It's a lovely evening, isn't it? Is your father in?"

Little Rodney doesn't know how to respond. He walks over to Diggman to make sure there's nothing visibly wrong with him. The old man straightens up and turns around, and Little Rodney can see he looks better than ever. But Big Rodney dropped in on Diggman before he left, and the old man already knew he was going to London.

While Little Rodney's back is turned, Isaac manages to sneak up on him. He feels a hand on his shoulder and almost knocks Isaac down as he recoils in shock. When he sees who it is, he settles down a bit. But not a lot.

"What are you doing here?"

"Just thought I'd come by. Drop in. Just drop right by. If you're not busy. Not too busy. I know you've been up at night. And I've been working nights too. So I'm all frazzled. All out of whack. Got my days and nights all jumbled, you know?"

"Right. Well. Do you want to come in?"

"Sure. Sure. Sure. Positively. Yup. Yup. Yup. It's a funny one. This one. This job. You know? Real strange one. It's-"

Isaac loses his train of thought as they enter the big house and see Rocky. He is sat at the dining table, surrounded by scraps of paper and small plastic tokens. At the centre of the table is the board. Though it's been a long time since he last saw it, Little Rodney instantly recognises *Infection*, the magnificently complex game that Rocky created and spent three years perfecting. It would appear that Rocky has been sat here all night, and Little Rodney is suddenly filled with remorse, realising the gravity of the situation.

"Rocky? Rocky? Hey."

Rocky doesn't say anything. He doesn't move. They try prodding him, but it seems nothing can get his attention. They try waving their hands in front of his face which only agitates him, causing him to make little groans of protest. He moves the counters here and there and jots notes on the scraps of paper.

"What is all this then? All this stuff? All these bits?"

"It's complicated."

Rocky nods. "You can say that again," he mumbles.

"You've got to get ready for the show, Rocky."

The boy scrunches up his face and shakes his head and waves them away.

"Shit." Little Rodney says. "I didn't think I'd actually have to do it. I'm going to have to bloody well do it!"

"The show? You can do the show. You can do it! I believe in you. I have faith."

"Isaac, do you know how to work the control thingy?"

"I can try. I can do my best. My darn best. My absolute maximum best effort."

"Shit."

Little Rodney shuffles through stacks of papers to find the script that his father lined up, while Isaac plays with settings on a small control panel.

"How long have we got?" Isaac asks.

"Seven minutes. Will you be ready?"

"You know it. For sure. Most certainly. Yes."

Little Rodney finds the right script and scans its content. He tries mimicking the way Rocky speaks, but can't get it right. Isaac is looking at him, concerned.

"Five minutes."

"Right. OK. Let's do it."

Little Rodney sits in the chair, which is set much too high for him. He wonders if he has time to readjust it, and changes his mind several times on the matter.

"Two minutes."

He decides he doesn't have time. He sits awkwardly and breathes heavily until Isaac gives him a slight nod.

"Hello. Uh, good evening night owls. This is Restrained Rodney's Bedtime Broadcast. I'm Rodney. Obviously not *the* Rodney. I'm a different Rodney. I'm his son, actually. So. Yeah."

Isaac has his head in his hands, but manages to give Little Rodney a sympathetic thumbs up.

"OK, we're going to kick things off with a little song. Well, just a song, really. A regular sized song." He snorts a nervous micro-laugh and looks again to Isaac who still has one thumb up.

"This is The Busboys with their new hit, 'Wipedown'." The song plays and Little Rodney starts shaking. He feels a lump in his throat and knows that if he has to talk again he'll certainly crumble.

"Right. OK. That wasn't perfect. That wasn't absolutely ideal. But it was- It was what it was. It is what it is. OK. It's gonna be fine. Just breathe."

Little Rodney takes slow breaths and on every exhale his lip quivers and his eyes start to fill with tears.

"Come on, Rodney. Pull yourself together. Get your act together. Pull your act right the way together. Come on. Just, here. Look at this script. Look, next up is this bit. Right here. This bit just right here. This about the Blackout. That's written out. It's written all the way out. You don't even need to think of anything. That's there. Then after that it's straight to the clip and that's another break. That's the end of that bit and we're closer to the end, right? Right? All righty? Just breathe. In. Out. In. Out."

As The Busboys sing their second chorus, Little Rodney calms down.

"You're right. Thanks Isaac. I'm fine. It's going to be fine."

The song fades out, and Little Rodney takes another deep breath.

"Again, that was The Busboys with 'Wipedown'. Tonight we will once again be taking a deep dive into the darkness, as we revisit some key moments from the Blackout. It put people out of business, saw massive rise in crime, and made listening to the radio the nation's favourite pastime. Even as the light returned, shows hosted by Restrained Rodney, Dame Harriet Henrietta Harrison, God rest her soul, and of course Rambunctious Rico, all continued to gain popularity. Here are a couple more clips from those famous broadcasts, this first one is from Dame Harriet. Incidentally, this segment aired exactly eight years before her tragic death, when Dame Harriet and her horse, Algernon, were struck by a rogue hot-air balloon."

Little Rodney plays the clip, sighs with relief, and smiles. He turns to Isaac, who looks back in shock, a single tear rolling down his cheek.

"Algernon died too?"

As the show goes on, Little Rodney becomes more comfortable. Isaac even manages to work out how to use the phone lines for the planned competition. A woman in

Durham wins a signed copy of *Silent Cries (From Blackened Eyes)*.

"Can you see how many people are listening?" Little Rodney asks Isaac while a man from Somerset talks about how he lost his job at the premium lard manufacturing company.

"We're at around seven million."

"That's good, right?"

"Yeah, it's only down a bit."

"What do you mean down a bit?"

"Well it looks like when Rocky was presenting, it was getting a few hundred thousand more."

"You're shitting me?"

"And, of course, when your dad was on it was much higher."

They wrap up the show and go upstairs, where Rocky still sits at the dining table. He looks dreadful, pale and sweating. His eyes are red and he's shaking profusely.

"You've got to go to sleep, Rocky."

The boy dismissively waves his hand.

Little Rodney goes into the cupboard and grabs some mushy peas, which he knows Rocky loves. He feeds them to him, making sure the spoon doesn't enter his line of sight for fear of agitating the boy. Rocky swallows the spoonfuls whole. Isaac goes back to telling

Little Rodney about his new job, as though the last eight hours hadn't happened.

"It's a madhouse down there. Bonkers. Never seen anything like it. There's loads of us. Hundreds. Just in the one office. And it's non stop. I hardly even get the chance to talk to anyone. And you know me. I like to make friends."

Little Rodney isn't listening. He's watching Rocky make notes on the scraps of paper, creating new characters and settings for *Infection*. Rocky writes about someone called Miguel, who wears an eyepatch and uses a different weapon for every kill.

"There's whisperings. Little rumours going around. About the stuff that's going on behind the scenes. Behind closed doors. There's something really quite sinister happening there. Real shady. A new government contract. An arrangement they have with Dignity."

The phone rings. Little Rodney hands the bowl of peas to Isaac, who is still trying to tell his story. He obstructs Rocky's view with the pea-piled spoon, which angers the boy. He groans and knocks Isaac's hand away, tossing peas everywhere.

"You know, they make out it's only the mega-rich who use Dignity. But it's not like that. Not any more."

"How was the show?" Big Rodney asks from the other end of the line.

"It was fine."

"Good good."

Little Rodney notices something strange in his father's voice. He sounds withdrawn. Little Rodney's stomach tightens and he wonders whether he has been caught out.

"Can I have a chat with Rocky?"

He looks over to Isaac and Rocky and the piles of papers, pens, and peas on the table.

"He's already left. I think he's starting to take the strain. Wanted to get some rest."

Big Rodney says nothing for a while.

"Aunt Rita died."

"Oh?"

"It was all very sad, Rodney. Really sad. She wasn't right. You see how bad it looks on the news but then you see it for yourself and it really is very bad. It's grim."

Little Rodney doesn't know what to say. He's never heard his dad speak like this. Even after his mother's incident.

"Anyway, I'm going to be coming back, I suppose. Uncle Ivan said he doesn't even want a funeral for her. What's that all about?"

Little Rodney takes a sheet of paper from the dining table and sits down to write his plan. Rocky is at the other end. He's sleeping now, with his head on the table and a pen still resting between two loose fingers. He's completely silent. Little Rodney has to lean close to make sure he's still breathing.

Isaac comes in from the other room, having slept on the sofa.

"Best sleep I've had," he says. "Tremendous stuff. Great stuff."

Little Rodney gives a nod and goes back to his notes.

"You've not been up all this time, have you?"

"No, no, no. I only just got up myself. Rocky was out when I came down."

"Oh, good. Very good. Very very good." He's whispering now, and exaggeratedly tip-toeing around the kitchen.

"You're alright, you know? I don't think he's waking up any time soon."

"What are you writing?"

"I'm coming up with stuff for the show."

"Aren't there any more scripts?"

"This is my last chance before dad gets back. I want it to be a good one. I want those ten million listeners."

"And how do you suppose we do that?"

Isaac counts down on his fingers, keeping an eye on the ratings on the screen in front of him. He looks towards Little Rodney, with one finger up, then a closed fist.

"Good evening, night owls. This is Restrained Rodney's Bedtime Broadcast. I'm Little Rodney. A lot of you have been asking where Restrained Rodney is. Well, he, like many of us, has a dear friend who is suffering from the Sadness. It's been five months since the first victims of this supposed case of mass hysteria were reported. On this show we'll be talking to you about your experiences with this sinister phenomenon. We'll also be talking to a special guest, who prefers to remain anonymous, about his role within the private medical company, 'Dignity', and about their strange response to the psychogenic illness."

Little Rodney improvises from the notes he's made. He feels, for the first time, completely in his element. He goes through the documented facts around the Sadness, reading out clippings from newspaper articles, stories about the school where the first cases occurred. The teenagers who were found catatonic, staring into space, sometimes screaming, sometimes silent. He talks about towns in which the population has been decimated. He talks about the strange way in which all these events don't seem to be causing notable panic. Most people are going on with their lives. The surveys which show that most Brits aren't any more anxious than they were this time last year. He takes calls from people in Leeds and Leicester and

Liverpool. People who have lost husbands and wives and brothers and sisters and mothers and fathers. One woman talks calmly to Little Rodney while someone else on her end is screaming. She says it's her neighbour. She says she's complained to their landlord, but there's nothing he can do. She says she's just going to have to wait until the neighbour either loses her voice or dies.

"How are the numbers looking?" Little Rodney asks, during an advert for a new kind of window cleaner.

"They're way up. Up, up, up. We peaked at almost nine million when that woman was talking about her brother who couldn't stop dancing."

"God rest his soul."

"God rest his soul."

"How long have we got left?"

"Twenty minutes."

"You still reckon you can do the interview."

"Sure, sure, sure. No doubt. Absolutely."

Isaac raises his hand to signal that the adverts are about to finish, and switches on his own microphone.

"Just before we hand you back to Rambunctious Rico, we have one more person to speak to. He's in the studio with me and though he wishes to remain anonymous, we can say that he works inside the Dignity offices here in Chesterfield. As such, he has insider information that I believe should be made public. Let me introduce this guest, who I will refer to as Joe. How are you feeling Joe?"

"I'm feeling good. Real good. Well, mostly good. It is, of course, a very serious matter. Very serious. Very important."

"Now, am I right in thinking that there's been a lot of whisperings at the Dignity offices as to what the company is getting up to in these troubling times?"

"That's right. That's absolutely right."

"An air of paranoia, you might say?"

"That is something you might say. It's something I might say. It's something lots of people might say."

"Can you elaborate?"

"I can elaborate, Rodney. That's something I can definitely do. I won't say exactly how long I've worked at Dignity. But it's been long enough to see that something is amiss. I know that won't be giving anything away to my employers because, honestly, they have new people coming in every day."

"How many?"

"Very many."

"Ten?"

"At least!"

"Twenty?"

"At most."

"Between ten and twenty?"

"That's right."

"Interesting."

"Interesting is a word you might use. And you'd be right to use it. Because it is. It is interesting. 'Why the sudden increase in new employees?', you might ask."

"I was going to ask."

"I sensed that you were. That's why I brought it up."

"It's like you can read my mind."

"Would that it were so simple. Now, as we all know, Dignity's usual clientele tend to be those who are both severely depressed and incredibly rich. It's an expensive service. But what if I told you that in the last month or so, they've been assigned by the government to use their services on people who, not only can't afford it themselves, but who aren't even aware that the process is taking place?"

"If you told me that, Joe, I'd say you're a crazy person. But after I'd had some time to process it, I might ask you how you became aware of this."

"It would be a pertinent question, Rodney. Now, I must confess that this is mostly speculation. And, of course, Dignity has always been somewhat secretive. But, essentially, they have always had a paying customer who wanted to die. Someone who was able to make their wishes plain both in terms of the euthanising and the memory-erasing. However, in these supposed new cases, the people are being chosen not by loved ones but by government agents."

"So what's the implication here?"

"The truth is, I'm not sure. Are the government erasing people they deem 'undesirable'? I don't know. Are they taking out spies? Terrorists? Criminals? I don't know. Are they, perhaps, underplaying the true extent of the Sadness by making it appear that a huge number of victims never suffered from the illness and, in fact, never existed at all?"

There are sounds coming from upstairs. The creaking of doors and the shuffling of footsteps.

Little Rodney looks around just in time to see his father come down into the basement wearing an expression of disappointment and disbelief.

"Only time will tell." Isaac says, before quickly fading both their mics down and setting up a song to play.

"What's going on? Who gave Rocky the game? What's Isaac doing here? Why are you doing the show? Why didn't you call me? What the shitting hell is going on?"

Isaac looks at Little Rodney, and Little Rodney looks at the ground.

"Everyone upstairs."

"But what about the show?"

"The show is done. Everyone upstairs. Now."

Big Rodney leads them outside so they can talk without waking Rocky, who still has his head in his hands on the dining table. Little Rodney can hardly bare to look at his father. He occasionally glances up to see Big Rodney looking tired and upset. He half expects his father to burst into rage or burst into tears at any moment. But Big Rodney takes a deep breath and stands facing the boys with his hands on his hips.

"Uncle Ivan died." He says. "Just before I left. He was sad about Rita, obviously, but he was alright. He was fine. Then he just-"

Big Rodney looks away from the boys. Now everyone is staring at the sky.

"Is Rocky bad?"

"Yeah."

"I don't suppose it really matters."

In searching for somewhere else to look, Big Rodney sees Diggman walking towards them.

"Since when was Diggman up and about?"

The old man stops and nods at each of them.

"Very good show." He says to Big Rodney.

"It was Little Rodney."

"I see. It's turning into a nice little family business."

Big Rodney looks at the old man, trying to recall something that's stuck in the back of his mind.

"Should we all go in for a drink?" He asks.

"I don't see why not." Says Diggman.

So Big Rodney, Little Rodney, Isaac and Digmann all go to the big house. Isaac quietly makes hot chocolates while father and son attempt to pack the game away without disturbing Rocky.

So they can speak freely, they all walk out to the front of the house. In the end, though, none of them has much to say. They sip their drinks, and watch intently as three suited men come slowly trudging towards them through the muddy field. No one calls out to the men. They're still a ways away.

SCOUTS

The man's wife scrambles eggs that she took
from the chicken coops in Mrs Barrett's garden.
The man is stood out front, surveying the
street. He sees his neighbour sat in a deck
chair, reading a two month old newspaper. His
neighbour waves, but the man doesn't wave
back. He keeps his hands on his hips. He
shakes his head and puffs his cheeks out as if
to say, 'here we go again'. The neighbour rolls
his eyes and smiles.

   For the first time in a long time, the
street looks perfectly clean. It's almost as
though nothing had happened. They finished
clearing the last of the scattered bric-a-brac
from outside Mr Berwick's house yesterday.
Though Mr Berwick was one of the first to
leave, they didn't want to get too close while
his dog was still there. The man, his wife, and
their neighbour had all individually considered
going over to feed the dog. But they knew what
the dog was like, and they didn't want to run
the risk of getting bitten or worse, especially
since the doctor left town. The dog died on
Thursday. It had been crying out for some time,
and the man briefly felt guilty. But, of course,
he had bigger things to worry about.

The man waters his plants and checks on his broad beans. He has more vegetables planted in the gardens of the two houses either side of him. The man, his wife, and their neighbour make use of almost every house on the street. It's like they own the place. They will often get together to have their tea at number four, number eight, or, if they're feeling adventurous, number two. Sometimes they all sleep in one room of one house, or different rooms in different houses. The man, his wife, and their neighbour are all the best of friends.

Of course, before all this happened, the man and his wife never really spoke to their neighbour. They thought he was a strange young man. When they saw him posting signs in his windows warning of bizarre conspiracies and covert government plans, they assumed he was crazy. When they finally got to know him they found they were right, but also that he was ultimately harmless. He has some unsavoury political opinions that differ greatly from those held by the man and his wife, and he is occasionally prone to sudden outbursts of paranoid ranting. But the man's wife, more often than not, can subdue him with apple crumble or jam tarts.

The man and his neighbour both hear the faint sound of moaning, but neither of them react to it. They just pray it stops before whatever it is gets close enough that they have to act. But the moaning grows louder and they soon realise something is heading their way. The man and his neighbour instinctively look up to the top of the street and see Mrs Battersby. She's got her brand new motorised wheelchair on full 'hare' setting, and she's bolting towards them. Tears are streaming down her cheeks. She's wildly shaking her head and crying out as though in great physical pain. The man and his neighbour watch on, dead-eyed, as she reaches the end of the cul-de-sac, loops around, and gets halfway back up the street before coming to a sharp halt. She spins in circles for a moment before throwing herself from the chair. She bashes her head against the concrete over and over. It's an awful sound, and the man decides that something must be done.

"What should we do?" He calls over to his neighbour.

"Throw her your shears."

He looks at the garden shears that lay beside him on the grass. He shakes his head, feeling nauseous at the thought of her cutting her own head off. All the while, Mrs Battersby keeps ramming her face into the ground. She wails until her voice gets hoarse.

"What's all this?" The man's wife says calmly, coming out the house.

"It's Battersby. She's on her way out."

The man's wife tuts. "Can't you throw her the shears or something?"

"I'll get my gun." The neighbour says, walking to his front door with no particular urgency.

The man and his wife exchange looks. They didn't know their neighbour owned a gun. The man has never even seen one. Not in real life. The neighbour soon comes back, holding the weapon. He steps through his gate, places it on the ground, and kicks it over to the old woman. When she sees it, she eagerly crawls over, picks it up and without hesitation, tries to shoot herself in the head. The gun, however, makes no sound. Not even a click.

"Shitting hell, the safety's on."

Mrs Battersby manically tries and tries again to shoot herself. The neighbour walks over and attempts to pry the gun out of her hands. It's not easy, and she doesn't take kindly to it. She holds on tight with one hand and slaps the neighbour with the other. When he does manage to overpower her, she goes back to smashing her head on the concrete. The neighbour fiddles with the gun for a while, struggling to remember how it works. He gets the safety off and tries to hand it back to the neighbour but she's uninterested. She's crying and flailing. In the end, the neighbour grows tired of waiting. He turns his head away and shoots the gun. It gets her in the stomach. Her cries become somewhat muted, but she is still alive. He shoots her again just below the eye, and she finally shuts up.

"What a kerfuffle." The man's wife says.

The man remembers his uncle telling him once how guns are louder than you'd imagine. But, perhaps because he had that stuck in his mind, the sound ended up being just like he'd imagined. If not quieter. Especially when compared to the tortured screams that had come before.

The man, his wife, and their neighbour spend some time looking at Mrs Battersby. They form a circle around her in the middle of the street. The neighbour gets in the motorised wheelchair, switches it to 'tortoise', and rides it over to Ian Crabtree's driveway, next to a BMW the neighbour took from an abandoned auto repair shop.

"Don't just stare at her, love." The man's wife says. "Go get the priest and I'll finish breakfast."

"Oh, do I have to?"

The man's wife gives him a stern look, so he knows he has to. He turns to his neighbour who sits in the wheelchair, smoking. He gives the man a sympathetic look, but doesn't offer to tag along.

The man won't take the car, though it's a long walk. He and his neighbour are only part way through clearing a big pile up of vehicles on the main road that leads to the next town over. He doesn't feel like tackling any of it on his own. It's a joint project.

To get to the priest's house on foot, he has to pass through a dense wooded area. It's rare that you can get through it these days without finding a dead body or two, often hanging from the trees. This time, though, the man thinks he might get away without encountering anything.

Just before he's out of the woods, he sees what he thinks is a body out the corner of his eye. But as he turns round, he finds it's a living teenage boy. He wears only his underpants and a pair of glasses. He's stopped moving mid-step, so that he looks like a picture of a Bigfoot sighting. He carries a bouquet of flowers, which the man quickly realises must have been taken from one of trees. Sometimes people will leave them here when a loved one is found in the woods. The idea of this disturbs the man. It's not so much that he thinks it's disrespectful, but more that he thinks someone should probably do something about it. And since he's the only one around, he knows it has to be him. But as soon as he takes one step towards the boy, the boy darts off. The man doesn't chase him, but marginally increases his walking speed so that it might look, if anyone was there to see it, as though he is making an effort.

The boy runs far out of sight, but the man still follows in the same direction for a little while. He soon comes across a campsite. There are a couple of tents, half taken down and some plastic bottles and food wrappers scattered around. There's a leather belt, which he picks up. Attached to the belt are several bottle caps that have been made into pin-badges and painted different colours. Uninterpretable symbols have been drawn onto them. He takes the belt with him as he heads back in the direction of the priest's house.

The priest is old, older even than the man. The man doesn't know for sure, but would guess that the priest is well into his 90s. He has more wrinkles than anyone would care to count and dark purple patches under his eyes. He communicates mostly in noises. Grunts and groans of disapproval and, on rare occasions, approval. When he's confused or indignant, he makes a questioning noise, a rising, rattling, honking yawn that drives the man crazy. He makes a particularly displeasing variant on this noise when he sees the man hasn't brought his car. Though, for his age, the priest gets around just fine. He walks faster than the man, who likes to move at a leisurely pace.

By the time the man and the priest get back to the street, the man's neighbour has already dug a grave for Mrs Battersby in the Mosleys garden. The man helps him lower the body and refill the hole. The man's wife lays flowers and a small wooden sign on which she has etched 'Mrs Battersby'. The priest groans, apparently saying a few words which somehow the man's wife is able to understand. She nods along and sheds a tear after a particularly heartfelt grunt.

"He knew her well." She says to her husband.

She suggests that they take turns saying something themselves. This is easy enough for her. The man's wife was a churchgoer like Mrs Battersby and was able to talk about how well she played the organ and about her grandchildren in Canada.

"I often saw her at the big Tesco," the man's neighbour says, "she would shout at the teenagers on the checkouts who were always hungover and rude. Always doing the lord's work." The man's wife and the priest nod.

The man doesn't remember ever meeting Mrs Battersby, but his wife insists he say a few words.

"She really must have loved that wheelchair. Who wouldn't? It's nice to think that maybe she's riding that great motorised wheelchair in the sky."

No one looks happy with this sentiment, but they all say a prayer and retreat back to the house of the man and his wife.

The man, his wife, their neighbour and the priest all sit around the dining room table. The man and the priest eat soup made by the man's wife, with slightly stale bread she took from Ray's bakery three days ago, just after Ray succumbed.

"Well don't you think it's a bit strange?" The neighbour asks the priest.

"Some people, they get it and die within minutes. Some people stick around for days. Some people, like us, are showing no signs of it at all. I mean, what kind of illness is this anyway?"

The priest grunts. The man keeps his eyes to the soup.

"I'll tell you what it is. It's a conspiracy concocted by the liberal elite. They'll get us all if we're not careful."

The priest chuckles, which the neighbour doesn't seem to like one bit. The man and his wife have stopped trying to argue with their neighbour on this topic. Whenever they tell him that it's not a healthy way to think, he simply reminds them that he's the one who has three years' worth of supplies in a bunker below his house. Something that now seems very useful.

In an attempt to prevent the neighbour working himself up into a frenzy, the man suggests they take stock of who is left.

"Mr and Mrs Keogh." The man's wife says. "Miss Cole and her mum."

"Mr Marybourne."

"No, Mr Marybourne died on Tuesday."

"Oh dear."

"I never cared much for Mr Marybourne."

The priest makes a series of groans.

"That's right," says the man's wife, "the Anderson boys are still around."

"But the Andersons died weeks ago. Who's looking after them?"

The priest grunts.

"I see."

"I saw a boy when I was out."

"You did?"

"Blonde, glasses, about thirteen or fourteen."

"Could be Billy Harricks?"

"He ran off when he saw me, but there was a campsite nearby so maybe there's a few of them out there."

"So there's us four, the Keoghs', Miss and Mrs Cole, Timmy and Tommy Anderson, and Billy Harricks."

The priest moans.

"Of course!" The man's wife says. "Well we can check on him tomorrow."

"Check on who?"

"The Father's brother. I don't want him to think he's been forgotten out there."

"Good luck," says the neighbour. "He's a piece of work."

The man sits upright, suddenly alert, in the bed that once belonged to Mr and Mrs Smith. His wife sleeps soundly next to him. It's three in the morning and he can hear sounds coming from outside. He goes to the window but it's too dark to see much of anything. When he opens it up he hears two people speaking to each other. They're quiet, but not whispering.

The man goes out in his dressing gown and sees that the BMW his neighbour drove the priest home in is still gone. He makes his way towards Mr and Mrs Mosley's garden. He shines a torch on the grave of Mrs Battersby and notices that the flowers his wife left are gone. Hearing a scuffle by the fence, he turns his light towards two boys, Tommy Anderson and the boy who might or might not be Billy Harricks. They briefly stop moving, caught in the light, but quickly return to their attempts to scale the fence. Billy makes it over easy, but Tommy, still holding Mrs Battersby's flowers, doesn't, and hurts himself in the process. He falls back down onto the garden path, crying out while his friend's quick footsteps become distant echoes.

"Some mate."

"Bugger off, nonce." Tommy says through tears, holding his knee.

"Don't get cheeky. There's a first aid kit in the house."

"You can't paedo me, mate. Just try, see what happens."

The man hears the garden gate open and close and turns to see his wife, who has come to see what all the fuss is about.

"Miss, this man is trying to paedo me! Miss!"

"He was nicking flowers from Battersby's grave. His friend left him."

"Well let's get him inside."

The boy settles down somewhat when the man's wife suggests making him something to eat. He still complains about his knee, though, and gets the man to carry him inside. As he does this, the man realises that the boy is wearing a belt around his shoulder like a sash, similar to the one he had found in the woods. Tommy's belt, however, only has two of the bottle cap badges.

The man places the boy on Mr and Mrs Mosley's sofa and takes a look at his knee. Once he clears the blood away, he can see it isn't as bad as it had first appeared. The boy still cries, though, and acts as though he is unable to move, let alone stand. So the man sets a stool across from the boy where he can sit while his wife takes a loaf of bread from the freezer and a pot of jam from the fridge.

"What's with the belt?"

The boy stares at the man but says nothing.

"I found one just like it yesterday. In the woods."

The boy tries to act uninterested, but doesn't do a very good job of it.

"I'll need to take that off your hands."

"You will, will you? What is it?"

"It's a belt."

"I'd have never guessed."

"They're badges."

"They're bottle caps."

"Badges made from bottle caps."

"So what are they for?"

"I can't say."

"Where are your parents?" The man asks, and instantly regrets doing so. The boy cocks his head with the sympathetic look you might give to an idiot.

"I'm sorry."

"No you're not." The boy says.

"No, I suppose I'm not. Not particularly anyway. I don't know why I said that."

For a moment they are both silent. The only sound is the man's wife humming and spreading jam.

"The badges you found belong to the boy who was with me before."

"Billy Harricks? Is it just you two out there in the woods?"

"No."

"Who else?"

"Why do you care?"

"I'm just making conversation."

"There's ten of us. There was more but some left."

"Where did they go?"

"Can I take some food back to the camp? My leg feels better now. I can walk."

"With enough food for ten?"

"Yes."

"No."

After they've eaten their toast, the man fills the boot of his car with bags of food and drives the boy out to the woods.

The man parks his car and he and the boy walk for half an hour before getting to a small clearing with several tents and a fire. There are six boys sat in a semi-circle. The first to notice the man is a round kid with a wild mess of hair. He taps the arm of the boy next to him, who does the same to the boy next to him, until they're all looking at Tommy and the man.

"We got more food," Tommy says, and passes the bags around. The boys say nothing of the man, and unenthusiastically inspect the food.

"Billy and Lewis are off looking for you."
Says one boy.

"They'll be back soon enough, I reckon."
Says another.

Tommy introduces the man to the boys.
His brother, Timmy Anderson is there. There's
John Johnson, Jon Robson, Rob Johnston,
and Bobby Robinson. The round one is called
Greggs.

"There's also Ivan, who's sleeping, and
Billy and Lewis. They'll be back soon."

Just as Tommy says this, there's a rustle
in the bushes, and the two boys appear,
seemingly from within the bushes themselves.
Lewis looks to be the oldest of all of them. He
has little pube-like hairs above his lip and a
face covered in spots.

"What on God's green earth is this
nonce doing here?"

"He's no nonce," says Greggs, "he
brought us food."

"You'd let yourself get nonced for two
pasties and a Double Decker, Greggs."

"Really, he's fine." Says Tommy.

The man takes the leather belt he had
found and hands it over to Billy.

"Nice one, abandoning your friend with a
potential nonce."

"Definite nonce."

"You said there was nothing you could
do to help him." Lewis snaps at a suddenly

sheepish looking Billy. Lewis snatches the belt, and violently tears off one of the bottle cap badges. Billy huffs but Lewis gives him a stern look, and with a sigh of resignation, Billy turns away.

"What about the flowers?"

"You're not getting anything for them, either!"

Lewis has his own belt, which he wears over his shoulder. It's practically overrun with badges. They clatter against each other as he bends down to pick up one of the bags of food.

"Hardly fine dining." He says.

"I could always take it back."

Lewis doesn't respond. He turns to Billy once more, "Go put the flowers on the flower throne."

"Not if I'm not getting a badge for it."

"You'll have no badges at all if you don't."

Billy mutters something under his breath, picks up his flowers and walks off into the trees. Tommy takes the man's arm and urges him to follow, which he does, along with Lewis, Timmy, and John. They catch up with Billy, who is storming ahead, angrily swinging the flowers to and fro.

"Seriously, Billy, do grow up."

They soon reach another clearing. It's much darker out here, so Tommy and Timmy use a couple of torches to shine light on the flower throne which, true to its name, is an old armchair that is almost completely covered in different flowers. Resting on its seat is a blanket that is likewise covered in flowers. Billy and Lewis start working together to attach the individual flowers from Billy's bunch to bare areas on the chair's back and arms.

"If you get enough flowers for the flower throne, you get a badge." Tommy says. "Billy and Greggs are the only ones who don't have theirs yet."

"So what's the flower throne for?"

"Ceremonial purposes." Tommy recites, in a way that suggests he doesn't really know what this means. "It's quite uncomfortable, really. But you look pretty cool when you sit in it."

The sun is rising, and the man, without thinking about how he got into this situation, finds himself sitting down with the boys for food. Some of them seem unsettled by his presence. Particularly Lewis who stares the man down while they eat, with Billy and John either side of him doing the same. The rest of the boys enjoy their tins of beans with sausage chunks, not paying any mind to the man. Some of the kids drink beer, and they all smoke weed, which Lewis keeps a large supply of in a number of zip-lock bags in his tent. They offer the man a joint, which he refuses, and a beer, which he accepts.

"Aren't some of you too young to be drinking."

"We're all too young to be drinking."

The man finishes his beans with sausage chunks, and feels more satisfied than he has been in some time. He would have beans with sausage chunks as a child, and they haven't lost any of their appeal. He thinks they might actually be the best food there is. He says so to the boys, and they all agree. Even Lewis.

"The first time I got drunk, I was five." Says the man. "My dad was at work, and my mum was at the shops, and me and my brother took two beers out the fridge. I passed out. Obviously. Straight away. Mum was furious. She said, 'wait until your dad gets home'. I was so scared. But when dad got home, he just laughed. He found it really funny."

The boys like this story. He can see it in their red eyes. So he tells them more. He tells them stories about being young and going on the nick and picking up girls and then about being older and having to get a job and then being too old to do that. He tells them about the time he did a fart that lasted two whole minutes.

"Bullshit." Cries Greggs.

"I swear it's true."

"It can't be done. It simply can't be done."

"Not even for one minute."

"Bet you I can."

"Go on then."

The man closes his eyes, breathes deep, lifts a leg and breaks wind for exactly sixty seven seconds. John times it on his watch. The boys don't even cheer. It's beyond words. They're open mouthed, amazed, and deathly silent.

"A mighty wind, indeed."

"We have a badge for that." Tommy says.

Lewis looks to Timmy, who in turn looks to John.

"I approve it." Says John.

"I approve it." Says Timmy.

"The council approves." Says Lewis. "Get the man his badge."

John routes around in his backpack, stirring the clatter of a hundred bottle caps until he pulls out one that is dark green and hands it to the man.

"For disgraceful behaviour, I present you this badge."

"Thanks, lads. I'll treasure it forever."

"Greggs got that one for doing a massive shit. It was the size of a baby's head."

"It rained all day. It rained all night. And still, the shit remained."

"Astounding."

Greggs sits cross legged like a laughing Buddha and nods wisely.

It takes the man a very long time to get back to his car. He's tired and drunk but still he takes the dangerous drive home. When he stumbles in his wife is sat in the kitchen, folded arms and teary eyes.

"Where on earth have you been?"

The man only gets a couple of hours rest before his wife wakes him up again. She reminds him that he'd promised to visit the father's brother.

"I didn't promise anything. It was you who suggested it."

But, of course, the man's wife doesn't drive. Not since her car was crushed by a hot-air balloon some years back. A few minutes earlier and she'd have still been in the driver's seat.

Too tired and hungover, the man persuades his neighbour to drive him. They take the long way round, neither of them wanting to spend time clearing cars. They sit in silence, for the most part, until the man remembers something from the night before.

"What happened when you dropped the father off last night? Your car was gone for ages."

The neighbour chuckles. "If I told you, you'd never believe it."

"Try me."

"I saw a couple of kids walking into the woods on my way back."

"That's not so strange."

"There was something not right about them. They had all this weird get-up. They were acting very suspicious. And I overheard them talking about ceremonies and rituals."

"I don't know how good an idea it is to be following kids around in the woods."

"Well, I lost them pretty quickly anyway. But remember what I said to you before. A few weeks ago when we were having tea at number two."

"What happens at number two stays at number two."

"Yeah, yeah, yeah. Seriously, though. I said, it's these communist kids who are lasting all this out. They're not getting it like we are. They know something we don't, I'm sure of it. They're after us."

The man wants to set his neighbour straight, but knows that there's little he could say that wouldn't end up making the situation worse. What would his neighbour make of the flower chair, the badges, and the council?

They drive out to the edge of the woods and down a winding country road that leads to the house of the father's brother. The house had once been a grand and beautiful manor, but fell into disrepair long before the Sadness took hold. The father's brother once viewed the manor as an ambitious fixer-upper that still had value. Now, with what's happened, it's as worthless as the houses the man, his wife, and their neighbour move between.

When they knock at the front door to no response, they fear the worst. They separate, walking around either side of the house, peering through windows. It's the man's neighbour who finds him first. He spots two legs and half a torso flat on the floor, the rest of the body is out of his line of sight. He calls the man over, and together they decide to smash the window with a nearby brick. The man reaches through the broken window to open it up, and it's big enough for them both to get in.

The man and his neighbour stand over the father's brother. The man's neighbour wants to inspect the body, but admits he doesn't know what he'd be looking for. The man wonders when it happened. He thinks about how he slept in, and insisted on going the long way round. But he knows there is nothing anyone could have done.

After a brief discussion, the man and his neighbour decide that it would be best to take the body out into the garden and bury it. The man is confident that there will be a shovel in the old groundskeeper's shed out back. They wouldn't even need to fetch the priest. All things considered, the man thinks, it's not the worst way to spend an afternoon.

But when they attempt to pick up the father's brother's body, he suddenly springs into life and cries out in fear. Not the fear of a man with a crippling case of the Sadness, but the fear of a man who has woken up to find two men trying to bury him in his garden.

"Get your hands off me. You hear me? Put me down this instant!"

The shock causes the man to drop the father's brother's legs straight away. Luckily, the neighbour is more composed, and manages to gently lower the father's brother's head back onto the floor.

"We saw you through the window." The man's neighbour says. "Thought you were dead."

"Oh, yeah! Peeping, were you? Thought you'd come and pinch my valuables? Thought you'd snatch them from my cold dead hands?"

Looking around at the father's brother's 'valuables', the man finds it hard not to laugh. This room, as is the case for most of the house, is filled with piles of old newspapers, broken electrical appliances, and cardboard boxes stuffed with receipts, vintage porn mags, and empty glass bottles. He doesn't even have to look in the kitchen to know that there will be nothing but stacks of tinned peaches and half a tin of spam from 1996.

"Well you can bugger off now. Come back in a few weeks. Jesus, you might not even have to wait that long."

"Why are you on the floor?"

"I'm here for the view. Why do you think I'm on the floor? Are you simple?"

"You fell?"

"Ding, dong, we have a winner."

"Would you like us to help."

"Oh, no, no, no. I wouldn't want to put you out.

The man and his neighbour look at each other, shrug, and head for the front door.

"Where the bloody hell do you think you're going? Help me up, why don't you? I've been here two days already."

The man can't tell if the father's brother is exaggerating, but he can see that there are tins scattered around that once contained peaches, and an half-empty bottle of water. It smells bad in the room, but the man senses that this is most likely the way it always is.

They help the father's brother to his feet. He can't stand on his own, let alone walk, so they carry him over to his half-broken recliner in the corner. It's surrounded by more stacks of papers that are piled up to the arm rests. On top of the stacks are dirty knives and forks and mugs filled with mould. Hung above the chair is a picture of the father's brother with his wife and daughter. His daughter went missing three years ago. She would be thirty-two now. The man thinks her name is Judy. No one has seen the father's brother's wife in a long time. For all the man knows she could be hidden somewhere in the clutter.

The man's neighbour suggests bringing Mrs Battersby's motorised wheelchair over for him, and though the father's brother refuses, he says he'll do it anyway. They bring the father's brother some more tinned peaches and the phone in case of emergencies, then they take their leave. They can hear the father's brother grumbling, even when they're far from the house.

"That's right, just leave me here. Leave me here and don't bother checking in again."

As they sit in silence on the drive home, the man notices a change in his neighbours mood.

"Is everything alright?" He asks. His neighbour nods, half-heartedly.

This has happened before with the man's neighbour. Some time ago there was a period of a few days during which the man's neighbour stopped talking to the man and his wife. He would sit outside his house with an awful expression of seething hatred and anger. After three days of this, the man and his wife received a call in the dead of night. The doctor had found their neighbour in the town, crashing cars into one another, breaking windows, and setting fires in the middle of the street. Fortunately, their neighbour hadn't hurt himself, but the doctor wanted the man to come down to collect him. Within hours of the incident, the man's neighbour was back to normal, and nothing more was said on the matter.

"Are you sure everything's alright?" The man asks, once more. Again, his neighbour nods, this time with an accompanying hum. The man determines this is enough to put his mind at ease, and he soon drifts off into sleep, his head resting on the window.

When the man wakes up, he finds he is alone. He's still in the passenger seat of his neighbour's car, and the driver's side door is open wide. He steps out and looks around, but his neighbour is nowhere to be seen. He isn't far from his street, so the man decides to walk the rest of the way, in case his neighbour plans on coming back for the car.

The man's wife found seventeen boxes of tea bags in a nearby social club, and has brought them home with her. She has them stacked on the kitchen counter and looks at them with pride.

"That boy came back." She says to her husband as he comes through the door.

"Oh?"

"He had a couple of friends with him, too. A spotty one and a little fat one. You seem to have left quite an impression on them."

The man smiles which, in turn, makes his wife smile too.

"It was like they were here to see if you could come out and play."

His eyes open. It's dark now. His wife is stood by the window and he can hear strange noises.

"Come and see this." She says.

The man joins his wife and looks out to see John Johnson, Jon Robson, Rob Johnston, and Bobby Robinson carrying the flower chair down the street. Behind them is Timmy Anderson, Tommy Anderson, and Billy Harricks. At the back is Greggs, who carries a baby in his arms. The man realises this must be Ivan. Lewis is at the front, leading them in a chant.

"One of us. One of us. One of us."

Timmy, Tommy, and Billy have long branches in their hands and they're knocking them against the pavement as they walk. Lewis wears a Christmas cracker crown, and has his arms outstretched. Ivan, the baby, looks tired, but too interested in what's going on to sleep.

The man spends some time watching the boys as they make their procession up the street, before he spots his neighbour, crouched behind a bush outside his house. He wears a camo boiler suit, and his face is painted with dirt. He's holding his gun and looking up to the man's window. The man tries to call out to his neighbour, but he can't be heard over the chanting. The man's neighbour nods, as though he understands. But he doesn't understand. And the last thing the man sees before his neighbour jumps out from behind his bush is Greggs, lifting Ivan as high as he can, and the last thing he hears is the baby squealing with excitement and joy.

NOTHING WOULD MAKE ME HAPPIER

Richard wakes up at exactly the same time
every morning. It's the kind of structured
routine that his father would have admired,
were he here to see it. When he sleeps, he lies
flat on his back with his arms by his sides. His
ex-wife used to say it made him look like a
madman. She would later say that he really
was madman. But that had little to do with how
he sleeps. Or even how, when he wakes, he is
always instantly alert. He sits bolt upright in his
cold, metal-frame bed.

      There is hardly anything in this room.
Just Richard, the bed, and a long, large,
wooden crate in which he keeps all his clothes.
This includes several identical shirts, several
identical pairs of jeans and several identical
pairs of socks and pants. Richard has lived in
this remarkably small house for a little over five
years. He built it himself. It sits between a vast,
open field and a remarkably dense forest. It
took him a long time to find the location he
desired. He had his father's estate agent
working overtime. He had started to believe
such a place might not even exist. But he got
there eventually. You can walk three miles in
any direction and not come across a single

living soul. He has no TV. He has no radio. He is alone.

Richard washes and dresses and goes into the storage cupboard to get his first Nutri-Stick of the day. He has a lifetime supply of these small bars. His father invented them. They are cheap to make, contain everything a human needs to survive, and never expire. They could end world hunger, but no one wants to eat them. They taste so revolting that people would rather die. They did studies to prove it.

Across from the storage cupboard is another crate in which Richard keeps his art supplies. A stack of small canvasses, a few boxes filled with tubes of paint, and several brushes. He already has a canvas set up on an easel outside, on which is a half-finished painting of the landscape that extends beyond his front door. Wet grass and an overcast sky. Same as all the other paintings. This one, he feels, is destined to be his masterpiece.

When Richard paints he tries very hard to think of nothing, but inevitably ends up thinking of everything. He thinks about people. Billions of people making fools of themselves, behaving like savages. He thinks about how they might dress these days. What they might be saying about this or that. He thinks about how long it's been since he left. How long it might be until another election, another Olympics, another Eurovision. He thinks about what they'll discuss around their water coolers, on their trains, or in front of their televisions. He thinks about the think-pieces they will write and it makes his skin crawl. He never has to see these people, but the memory of them still prevents him from attaining the peace of mind he so desires. The memory of his unloving wife and idiot child who, unbeknownst to Richard, both died mere days after he left for his home in the woods. They were flattened by a falling piano on their way to the e-cig store, Vape Heaven, where they had planned to buy a present for the son's thirteenth birthday.

Richard snaps out of his daydream. His hand has been hovering over the canvas for some time. He looks off into the field and sees the fog rolling in. He thinks, not for the first time, that he can spot a figure off in the distance. He knows what fog can do to the mind. He closes his eyes and shakes his head, but when he opens them it's still there, clearer and clearer the longer he looks. He hears something. Something distinctly human. A whistle and a hum. He walks out from behind his canvas, edging further from his house. He hears it again, clearer and clearer and closer and closer. He holds his breath. Stands still for what seems like a very long time. Then it's gone. The figure vanishes, the sound stops, all swept away in the fog. He hurriedly walks back to his house, finding that he had walked father out than he thought.

While packing away his supplies, he realises things are not as they should be. There are tubes of paint here that he's sure he never brought out.

Then Richard sees it, and all the blood seems to rush from his body. He feels as though he's stood atop a very high building with nowhere to go but down. He feels sick and weak and dizzy. There's something on the canvas that wasn't there before. At the far end of the painted field, the silhouette of a man. Stuck, mid-step, as though making his way out of the picture.

Richard looks around, panicked. He tries calling out, 'who's there', but his voice breaks and hardly anything comes out. He can't move. His feet are glued to the ground and it's only with a tremendous effort that he finally manages to drag himself towards his front door.

Instinctively, he goes to his third supply crate. The one that contains survival and camping equipment. Gathering a few items into a large backpack, he finally composes himself enough to run back out and around the house, into the woods. He twists and turns, taking routes through the trees that only someone who has lived here as long as he has would know. He needs to be sure he isn't followed.

When he arrives at the clearing by the river, he hurriedly sets up camp, zips himself into his tent, and sits cross-legged, listening and listening and hearing only the running water.

***

Judy can't figure it out. Three days ago she thought her death was imminent, and hoped it would be swift. Every second that has passed since, she's been sure would be her last. At this point she's bored of it all and desperate for it to end.

She drags herself across the damp ground like a slug, blood trailing behind her. Occasionally she rests, and cranes her neck to look back at the mess she's left. It really is a lot of blood, she thinks. She's seen plenty in her time, but this really is excessive. She's startled she has any left to give.

"Come, now," she says, "This really is getting quite silly." Still, she crawls.

She can't imagine how far she has come, or how long she has been doing this. It feels like forever, but of course she is going very slowly. It must have been at least a few hours since she was able to walk, and even longer since she was able to run. She tries to tally it all up in her head, but can't make sense of it. She's sure, though, that she won't be able to walk again. Any travelling she has left must be done on her belly. Not that she knows where she is going. Ahead of her is a great expanse of nothing but fog. So, determined that this must really be the end, she commits herself to one final heave forward and then stops altogether, allowing herself to relax completely. It's briefly comforting, but once the adrenaline wears off, the pain rushes in.

"Right, this is it." She says. "This is where I die."

But, of course, she said that a mile back. And a mile before that, too. Even in the car, she said it, loud enough so that her man might hear.

"This it it then, is it? I'm gonna die in a boot? The shitting boot of a shitting Kia Ceed? What a crock! What a load of bollocks! The humanity! The shitting humanity!"

In retrospect, he probably didn't hear her. He was singing along with the radio.

She lies there for several minutes before she turns her head and spots the hatch. It's been there all along and she hadn't noticed. It's not small enough to miss, either. A big metal door with a little window. She goes through the painful process of readjusting herself so that she can crawl over it. She bangs on the metal and knocks on the window. It isn't dirty or rusty and it doesn't look very old. She makes a vague attempt at opening it, pulling at the big handle, but it won't open easily, so she quickly gives up. She sees that there's a lock, and of course she has no key.

"That's OK," she says, "I didn't want to look anyway. No use. I'm just going to stay right here. I'm just going to stay right here and die." She listens to the silent response. "I said, I'm just gonna lie right here and bloody well die! And about time too."

A thought occurs to Judy, that she doesn't know how old she is. She must be around thirty, she thinks. At least thirty. Better than dying when you're a child. Worse than dying in middle age. She doesn't know whether or not it's worse than dying as an old woman. All sick and decrepit. She'll never know for sure. "All in all," she says, "as far as dying goes, right now seems fair to middling."

She feels very tired now, and she decides she would like to close her eyes.

"Oh, I don't know."

She lets herself drift off, and it feels just like taking a well earned nap.

***

As he lies awake in his thin sleeping bag, in his small tent, shivering from the kind of cold you feel down to your bones, Richard thinks about everything.

He thinks about David Farmer's hundred lawnmowers. The biggest lawnmower collection in the western world. He thinks about the lawnmower conventions, admiring Hyundai, Mountfield, and Black & Decker. Hand propelled rotary petrol lawnmowers. Autocharging robotic lawnmowers. Cordless and brushless, ride-ons and rough cutters. David's face, grotesque with passion, talking about lawnmowers all day, every day. Richard would say, 'Why, David? Why always with the lawnmowers? Can't you see the lawn is mowed? The lawn can be mowed no more. Why can't you get a real hobby, David?' And he thinks about how much this pained David to hear, because, of course, David thought very highly of Richard. David wanted Richard to like him, ever since he was just a ruddy-cheeked child with only shears and a dream. So David stopped talking about lawnmowers, even though it was hard because he found them so very exciting to talk about. And after that, he hardly spoke to Richard at all.

And while Richard thinks about David Farmer, he also thinks about his cousin, Joe Croxley, who was accused of having intimate relations with a rooster on the Isle of Man. And how Joe was always adamant that he wasn't having intimate relations with said rooster, and everyone in the family chose to believe him. Everyone except Richard. And it was frustrating to Richard because they always said Joe was a horrible, nasty piece of work but in this case, when they had confirmation that he really was a horrible, nasty piece of work, suddenly it's all, 'he wouldn't do that' and 'he's just a bit strange'. And in the end, it was Richard they were angry with, simply for saying that he probably did have intimate relations with the rooster. And, of course, when it turned out that the people of the Isle of Man had enough evidence to confirm he definitely did have intimate relations with the rooster, still the family found ways to excuse it. And Richard would ask, 'why are you defending him?' And they would say, 'he's family'. And after that they hardly spoke to Richard at all.

And while Richard thinks about David Farmer and Joe Croxley, he also thinks about Grandmother Thyme. She had a plastic surgery addiction. She looked horrific, but her husband wouldn't acknowledge it. Not even behind her back. 'She looks like a monster!' Richard would say. Not to her grotesque face, of course. But to her husband and to other people. And they would gasp and declare, 'you can't say that!' And Richard couldn't understand this. He understood why she wanted the surgery; she had looked bad before. He had no problem with her getting whatever surgery she wanted. But it seemed crazy to him that, in private conversations, no one would admit that her surgeon was clearly not a talented man. 'We can all see it,' he would say, 'even she must see it. She owns mirrors. Her eyesight is fine. She's freakish. It's not up for debate. The woman is a disgrace. An ugly, horrible, stupid, disgrace. And everyone's just going to pretend she's not?' And Richard would plead with her husband, saying, 'It just doesn't add up. Surely you know it's fine. It's fine that she's ugly and horrible and stupid because she has people like you and I. People who are going to be nice to her regardless. But why not acknowledge it when she's not around? Why not share? We're just patient people who suffer through having to look at this woman's hideous visage'. And after that he hardly spoke to Richard at all.

And all this thinking is exhausting to the point where it sends Richard to sleep. And when he wakes up, bolt upright and alert, it takes him a moment to remember where he is and what is going on. And the memory of the night before makes him feel stupid and crazy. And though he chuckles to himself, deep down he still feels unsettled.

It is several minutes past the time he would normally wake. Though, of course, he doesn't realise this.

***

"Oh, come on!" Judy cries, waking up again, still lying by the hatch in the field. "This is absurd."

It is dark now. She feels very different somehow. She puts her hand to the wound on her side and is startled to find it isn't damp. She's even more shocked when she realises she is wearing different clothes. She was wearing one of his T-Shirts and a pair of jeans and now she's wearing fresh pyjamas and a big puffy coat. These are her own clothes. From her own bag. Which, she's fairly certain, was in his car the last time she saw it. In this moment of shock and confusion, she jumps up to her feet. But this only begs more questions. How is she finding it so easy to stand? She lifts up her pyjama top and sees she's been bandaged up.

"You're here." She says. "You're following me. You're taunting me."

She can't see anything in the darkness of the field. But there's light coming from the window of the hatch. She tentatively taps on the hatch door with her foot. Then again, louder. Nothing happens.

She runs her hands across the grass, eventually landing on something. Her bag. Just a couple of feet from where she was laid. She opens it up and rummages through it for her torch. She shines the light on herself, confirming that she looks healthier and cleaner than ever. It must be him, she thinks. But this is so uncharacteristically kind.

She flashes the light to the ground and the first thing she sees is a key in the grass. She rolls her eyes, and curses her persistent good fortune. Sure enough, the key works, and the hatch door opens with ease.

Judy grabs her bag and cautiously climbs down the ladder. It leads to a concrete hallway, at the far end of which is another metal door which, in turn, leads to a brightly lit room. There's a sofa and tables and chairs. There are photos on the walls. She spends a while looking at them as though they were works of art. There's a stern looking man with a receding hairline who features in almost all the photos. In many of them he poses with a large woman who often has a cigar in her mouth. In some there's a small boy with a hare lip, dressed in a sailor suit.

"Is anyone there?" She calls out. There is no response.

She finds a bathroom, a bedroom, a kitchen, and a storage cupboard. Everything has been left neat and tidy. There's a radio attached to one of the walls with sprawling wires that go up and over the ceiling, out the metal door through which she came. She turns it on. A Busboys song is fading out and Restrained Rodney's Bedtime Broadcast is starting. But Restrained Rodney isn't there. It's a stranger, who sounds very upset about something. He's describing some awful tragedy which Judy assumes must be happening very far away.

"The streets are lined with bodies," the man says, "and people are walking through the city centre, unsure of who they are and how they got here."

It soon becomes apparent that the stranger isn't talking about somewhere very far away, but Manchester.

"Well that's no good." Judy says. She thinks about how much she'd like to be there. She doesn't know how she'd help, but she'd like to try. It's been so long since she was able to do something nice.

Only then does it occur to her that she doesn't even know where she is. For all she knows, Manchester could be within walking distance.

They had been in the car for hours. Then they walked together for what seemed like a full day. And that's saying nothing of all the time she spent running and crawling. She must be miles from Bideford. She looks around for any clues of where the bunker might be, but for the first time she has no luck. She thinks she's hit the jackpot when she finds a drawer full of letters, but the letters are addressed to different locations around the world. They all bear the name of a Mr Bradley Bradley, which makes Judy smile.

After a while, she begins to make herself feel at home in the underground apartment. She has a shower. She goes into the fridge and takes all the food she wants. She makes herself sandwiches. She pours herself glasses of orange juice. She changes into the men's clothes that she finds in the wardrobe. She lies on the sofa and flicks through magazines from the coffee table. She supposes that these are recent issues, but she can't be too sure. For a few hours it's as though she is a normal person, living a normal life. It's as though the man had never existed, and she'd never disappeared.

Inevitably, though, Judy can't help but think about what might be next for her. She has nowhere to go and no plan. What if Mr Bradley Bradley comes home? She remembers urban myths about people moving into houses and finding the old tenants living in the walls. The walls here are made of thick metal, so she thinks it unlikely. What if he's in a secret room, watching her? She, more than most, knows about the practicality of living in small spaces.

Her mind wanders and she stares at the ceiling for hours before turning to a clock on the wall to see that it is morning. She turns the radio on again and Rambunctious Rico is there, talking about all these awful things that are happening, not just in Manchester, but all over the country. She worries, but not for anyone in particular. She wishes she had someone she could worry about specifically. Instead, she worries and prays for every person in the world. She furrows her brow, and thinks about all the people who must be scared out there, who must be mourning so much loss and waste. Everyone, that is, other than her man. She couldn't care less what happens to him. The man who she believes could be waiting somewhere just beyond the hatch door or, God forbid, somewhere even closer.

***

Before going back to his house, Richard walks out to where he had seen the figure the night before. There is nothing and no one there, or any sign that anything or anyone was. He feels calm for a moment until he considers the fact that, if there really had been someone out in the field, they may have found their way to his house. They may be there now waiting for him. He tries his best to steady his nerves, knowing he'll be home soon to see for himself.

He walks straight past the painting he had left so hurriedly, letting himself in and cautiously tip-toeing through the house. He looks around and quickly assesses that everything is as it should be. Everything in its place. The storage cupboards closed, his bed still neatly made, his Nutri-Sticks uneaten. The weight of his fear is instantly lifted. He even starts to chuckle to himself, feeling a lightness he hasn't felt in a long while. In all the time he's lived here, and in all the time he spent preparing himself, he never thought he'd end up losing his mind. But here he is, imagining figures in the fog and ghosts painting themselves onto his canvas.

Still, even as he thinks about all this, there's a knot deep down in his stomach. The unshakable sense that something is not right. He buries the feeling and goes back outside to retrieve what he had left behind. He picks up the painting without looking at it, pretending to himself that some bird or cloud has caught his attention in that moment, and that his eyes are simply not drawn to the canvas. Feigning confidence that there would be nothing out of the ordinary there. He holds it at arms length, takes it inside, and places it against the wall, facing away from him.

But as the day goes on, the more he tries to act as though everything has returned to normal, the more that sense of dread and unease grows inside of him. His morning Nutri-Stick doesn't taste right. It doesn't look right, either. It's an unnatural colour. He's never noticed it before. It's a colour he doesn't think he's ever seen. He can't bear to finish it, so he folds the plastic wrapper over and puts it back in the cupboard.

He stays inside to paint, and sets up his easel in the centre of the room. But as he pencils yet another landscape, he can't help but feel it's all wrong. Is that what grass looks like? Is that a cloud? He looks at the paintings he finished last month but it all seems ridiculous. He peers out his window at the scenery and it's baffling. He steps outside, gets down on all fours and starts picking out individual blades of grass, holding them right up to his eyes. That can't be it. That's not normal. He takes another and another. He takes handfuls and holds them up to the sky. But the sky is not the sky he once knew. It's menacing and unfriendly. It's uncanny and sinister. It's a Rorschach test that he has been interpreting a certain way all his life, and now something fundamental has changed.

He gives up and puts everything away. He stands in the centre of the room staring at the back of last night's canvas. He knows there's a power emanating from it and it's driving him to despair. He tries moving it around the room in an attempt to put it out of sight and mind but his head always finds new ways to turn towards it. Eventually he loses the will to ignore it any longer.

He grabs the painting, holds it out in both hands for a moment, then turns it around. It is not as it was.

The silhouetted man is still there. And to his right is a woman. And behind her is another man. There are several people in the painting. Some, like the first, are vague shadows. But others are fully formed and detailed. A boy pushes an apple cart. A girl climbs a tree. A woman walks a dog. They are smiling and laughing. And they all look so happy.

***

Judy is bored. Unbearably so. She knows she should be used to this kind of thing, trapped underground with nothing to do and no one to talk to. This time, though, she's here of her own volition. She's done everything she can possibly think of to quell the boredom. The radio plays non-stop. It's the same thing over and over, more misery and misfortune and doom and dread. She's explored every room, looked in every cupboard, in every drawer, in every box and bag. She's taken inventory of every item in the bunker. She's examined every picture on the wall, took them down, and matched up faces. She's identified the man she believes to be Mr Bradley Bradley. He's the tall one with the goatee. She thinks he's very handsome, but also that he looks like he wouldn't be much fun. He has a blank expression across all the photos, and is almost always posed with his chin up, shoulders back, and arms straight by his sides. She's made up names for the other people she sees. The large woman she calls Big Fat Sandra and the sailor suit boy she calls Little Joe. She makes up stories for them, and imagines ways they might be related. She morns Big Fat Sandra, who she imagines dying of mouth cancer and gives a big congratulations to Little Joe, who she imagines becoming the sailor he always dreamed he would be.

She spends hours daydreaming, staring at the photos. She only snaps out of it when she hears a muted thud from somewhere above her. It makes the hairs on her arms stand up, and her heart sink. She feels cold and finds herself unable to move. She hears it again. She doesn't jump this time. She sits completely still on the sofa, all the pictures still scattered around her. She sits there for several minutes, not making a sound. Nothing happens.

With tremendous effort, she stands up, being as quiet as possible. Though she realises that the sound came from beyond the hatch. And it must have been very loud for her to have heard it at all. And, therefore, she would have to make a noise equally loud for anyone to hear her from out there. Still, she moves as stealthily as she can, taking shallow breaths through her mouth, stepping closer to the entrance of the underground apartment.

For the first time since she entered the hatch, Judy opens the door and pokes her head out to look around. It's not completely dark out yet, and she can see clearly, just a few feet away, several brown burlap sacks. She stares at them in fear for a while before it occurs to her that there's nothing particularly scary about them. She looks around and sees nothing else out of the ordinary. She climbs out of the hatch and inspects the sacks more closely. One is filled with rice, one with potatoes, one with canned foods, one with bottles of water, and one with various cereals, grains, nuts, and seeds. She stands over them for a minute, sure that someone must be lying in wait. When she is finally confident that she is alone, Judy takes the sacks down the hatch. Once they are all at the base of the ladder, she shuts the hatch door again and drags the sacks into the apartment, stacking them on the sofa.

She goes to the kitchen and makes herself a tea. From where she is stood she can see the back of the sofa. Only the tallest sack and a smaller sack on the arm rest are visible. It looks to her like a sack man is sat there.

"What brings you all the way out here?" She asks the sack man.

"I could ask you the same question."

"In all honesty, I'm not sure where 'out here' is."

"That makes two of us."

She goes over to the coffee table to turn the radio on.

"Hope you don't mind." She says.

Rambunctious Rico is in his final hour, and he sounds uncharacteristically shaken and choked up. He forces his words out, reading the evening news like it's the eulogy of a close friend.

"These. Are. Troublesome. Times. Indeed. And. Friends. If. You're. Still. Out. There. I. Hope. You're. Safe. And. I. Hope. You're. Keeping. In. Higher. Spirits. Than. I."

There is a moment of dead air. Judy knows these really are strange days.

"That's. All. For. Today. Goodbye."

More silence follows, where Restrained Rodney's Bedtime Broadcast would normally start. Judy listens for a long while. She tries turning it up and adjusting the dial. She wonders if the radio is broken. But she knows deep down it's not.

"It'll be alright."

"I hope so," says Judy.

"Have I ever lied to you?"

"Not that I know of. Can I be honest with you, Mr Bradley?"

"Please, Mr Bradley was my father. It's just Bradley."

"Bradley, I'm not sure anyone's coming to find me."

"That's as much of a good thing as a bad thing, though. Right?"

"I suppose. I would have liked to see mum again, in spite of everything."

"You're more forgiving than I would be in your situation."

"I try my best."

Judy hears another unfamiliar sound, different from the last. It's not quite as loud. A series of creaks and groans. Strangely, these noises don't fill Judy with quite as much dread, though she thinks her friend seems unsettled.

"What do you think that is?" Judy asks.

"I don't know, and I don't think we should stick around to find out!"

"We've got nowhere to go."

"Oh, God. We're trapped."

The creaks and groans grow louder, and they culminate in one big rattle and bang. Then, distinctly, footsteps. Coming up the corridor, towards the entrance of the apartment. The door opens, and a man stands there. A tall man, very slim, wearing a sailor suit. Mr Bradley Bradley looks nothing like Judy had imagined.

"Who the fuck are you? What are you doing here?"

Judy stutters, and doesn't manage to say anything that she would like to.

"Have you been eating my food? What are you doing with my photos? Who the fucking hell are you?"

"I'm Judy."

"Well will you fuck off, Judy?"

"I'd rather not."

"It wasn't really a question."

"It sounded like a question."

"Well, it was rhetorical."

"OK."

Judy quickly moves past Mr Bradley Bradley, and walks down the corridor, up the ladder, and back out into the field.

It's raining now. Judy feels like she could just lie down. She could carefully get down on her hands and knees and crawl until she finds a soft patch to curl up on. She feels something like a wave hit her, and suddenly she is tired. She is so tired of it all. Tired of moving and of living. She's more tired than she's ever been in her life. Even more than when she was running and crawling and walking for hours and hours. The open field around her becomes a haze. Everything is blurry. It's like she's under some sort of trance. She can't feel her arms or legs. She can't even see them. Only the blur and the bright shifting colours. The shades of green and blue. She can't move. She can't talk. The night comes and goes and she doesn't notice. Once or twice she remembers who she is and she screams so loud she thinks the whole world must be able to hear. And then she forgets again. And the night comes and goes. She doesn't feel hungry. She doesn't feel thirsty. She doesn't feel cold. She doesn't even feel tired anymore. She does feel something. Something in her throat, and in her chest, and in her stomach. Some great misshapen lump that moves through her and makes everything uneasy and uncertain and uncomfortable. The feeling that something isn't right. Something that should have been done has been forgotten and left to chance. Trouble is rearing its ugly head and there's not a thing she can do about it. And it's awful. And she knows that the moment she can pull herself together she's going to smash her head against that metal hatch door as hard as she possibly can and she won't stop until she's sure she wont have to feel this feeling ever again.

***

"Where are you?" Richard cries. "Who are you? What are you doing to me? Why are you doing this to me? How are you doing this to me?" He receives no response. He runs out into the field and finds nothing. Just the great green expanse as far as the eye can see. He can't look at it any longer. It empties his heart and his stomach. It fills him with a cold terror. So Richard turns around and runs back in the other direction, right past his little house, into the woods, through the dense trees, past where he had camped the night before. He runs down the riverside. He runs into parts of the woods he has never gone before. His feet get caught in tangles of weeds and roots and thorns, and he pulls them out as quickly, tearing his jeans and his cutting his legs. He runs and thinks about all the possible horrors that might await him were he ever to return to his little house. He thinks about all he has worked for as it turns wretched before him. He runs and thinks about how it couldn't last, and how nothing ever does. He thinks about moving far away, though he knows he couldn't possibly get any farther. He runs and thinks about David Farmer and Jim Croce and Grandfather Whatshisname.

And then he stops.

He stops and thinks some more. What was his name? His grandfather on his mother's side. Or his father's side. But he doesn't know his father. He doesn't think he's ever known his father. So it couldn't possibly be that. It must be his mothers father. And what did he do? What was his name? And who is Jim Croce? That's not right either. He thinks and thinks. He stands and thinks, and sits and thinks, and thinks out loud.

"David Farmer fixed cars. Jim Croce. Jim. Jim. James. James. That's not right."

He sits and thinks and chuckles to himself a little.

"I'm losing my mind. I'm losing my head here."

He sits and thinks and stays completely silent and completely still. He sees a squirrel scurrying up a tree. Richard is so still and silent that the squirrel doesn't even notice him there. So Richard just carries on watching for a while as the squirrel goes up and down and across branches. It occasionally stops to look around but never in the direction of Richard.

And as Richard sits and thinks and watches, he begins to feel as though he is a part of the woods themselves, indistinguishable from the trees. He sits and thinks and watches, still and silent. He does this until he forgets who he is and where he is. He feels so calm and free that it's a mystery to him how he ever managed to get so worked up in the first place. He knows he was upset about someone or something from his past. That he's sure of. But who? But what? But how? He doesn't even know anyone. He has no family, no friends. He's a man of the woods, and always has been. He likes it that way. He smiles wide and laughs loud. This startles the squirrel, who quickly scurries off. Richard doesn't mind.

There's a long, steep bank that leads to the water. Richard thinks about going down so he can sit there, under the shade of one of the trees. He doesn't give it much thought before he commits to the idea completely. He removes his shoes and socks and steps down cautiously. The grass is damp, and he doesn't like the idea of falling from this height. He has plenty to hold on to, though. He grips the tangled branches and long grass as he gently moves down, small step by small step. For the last couple of feet he lets go, and takes two big steps towards the bottom. But his foot gets caught on something that's hidden among the leaves, and he trips up. He falls down to the bottom of the bank and feels a sudden dull pain as his head hits a small rock that's embedded in the dirt. He lies there, feeling very funny and nauseous and cold. The shock of it all makes it hard for him to catch his breath. He puts his hand to his head. As he draws it back he sees blood.

He looks over to the other side of the river and notices a squirrel watching him. He wonders if it's the same squirrel. He likes to think it is. He tries to give the creature a smile as if to say that everything was alright. The squirrel gives no indication that he feels any particular way about it. But he watches Richard, perhaps just wanting to know what the man would do next.

Just as Richard feels himself drifting into unconsciousness, he sees the squirrel become very alert, and in an instant it is caught between the teeth of a fox. As the fox bites down on the squirrel, the creature makes a truly awful sound. Then, it is carried away. The fox moves steadily and without haste, downstream. And Richard is alone, newly aware of the harsh rushing of the river, and of the coldness and dampness of the ground beneath him, and of the ominous darkness of the clouds above.

Christy Smyth is a morbidly obtuse writer from Derbyshire, living in Merseyside. He is poor in money and poorer in spirit.

Acknowledgements

Richard, Mel, Jim Friel, Ma, Pa, Kieran, and Jess

For your patience, generosity, support, and encouragement

Ta x

OUR OTHER PUBLICATIONS

POETRY

The Devil Rides to Doncaster
by
Melody Clark

Frogs For Patti Smith
by
Louise M. Hart

FICTION

Too Dead For Dreaming
by
Richard Daniels

The Dark Earth of Albion
by
Gareth Spark

plastic-brain-press.com

Printed in Great Britain
by Amazon

63291221R00132